AVENGING ANGEL

AVENGING ANGEL

CAYCE POPONEA

Graphic Design
JADA D'LEE

WRITE HAND PUBLICATIONS

Copyright © 2019 by Cayce Poponea
All rights reserved.
No part of this book may be reproduced in any form or by any electronic or mechanical means, including information storage and retrieval systems, without written permission from the author, except for the use of brief quotations in a book review.
Printed in the United States of America
First Printing 2019

www.CaycePoponea.com

CHAPTER ONE

Willow bounced down the stairs the following morning, a new smile on her face as she passed the broken banister. Rounding the corner into the kitchen, she heard the voice of the man they introduced as Daragis. Unsurprisingly, he was upset to learn there wasn't enough Wolfsbane available to fill his current need, thanks to her pouring the majority of what they had on the shelves down the toilet when she returned early this morning. She had a plan on how to free her parents and by extension the other Factions.

Saige stood with her back to Willow, hands on her hips as she stared at the empty shelves where the Wolfsbane sat yesterday. She caught the tail-end of Daragis as he stomped across the street to the church, not bothering to hide where he was going as he'd done in the past. Now that Willow was free from the tiny bit of magic in the house, her eye were wide open to more than just a crumbling house.

"Willow, I need you to—"

"I know, Saige, I heard him. Let Brynn know I'll be in the greenhouse the rest of the day."

"Put extra love into it, Willow. Daragis will return in the morning and he expects a full crate."

Willow left the shop with a bigger smile while Saige mumbled under her breath about how she didn't understand where all the Wolfsbane disappeared to. Rounding the corner by the kitchen, she heard the sound of big band music coming from the library. Approaching cautiously, Willow peered around the edge of the door to see Brynn and Larkin holding one another tight as they slow danced to the music. She wished she had her phone, she would have snapped a photo to shove in their faces later when she called them out on their lies.

Slipping past the oblivious lovers, she headed to the back of the house where she'd opened all the windows early this morning, effectively killing every last stem of Wolfsbane in the room. Taking a sample of the roses she'd been nurturing back to life, she chanted a spell she'd memorized from her mother's spell book, watching with satisfied eyes as the red roses shifted to the purple-blue of Wolfsbane.

Hours later, Willow waited at the French doors in her room for Larkin to take his place on the ledge of the church. Minutes later, she witnessed him take a knee before shifting into his Gargoyle form. A quietly as possible, Willow tiptoed back to the stairs, tucking herself against the wall where she could see everything in the great room. As the clock in the hall struck eleven, the guards who escorted her down the street to the antique store, walk into the great room, a large bag in each of their hands. Standing in front is Vicktor, who is dragging what Willow can only assume is a Troll, based on never having seen one outside of movies, a thick shackle around its neck, wrists and ankles. The line stops beside the steps where Vicktor commands the Troll to hurry up, sticking him with a metal prod when he doesn't move fast enough. The poor Troll, who is now bleeding from Vicktor's spear, tapped out a pattern on the wall making the door open and bright light shine from within. Willow's birthmark began tingling as the Gargoyles disappear through the door, sacks in hand.

"Bingo," Willow whispered, before returning to her room, a triumphant smile on her face. Crossing her room, she pulled the curtain back, blowing an air kiss to Larkin before climbing between her sheets. She couldn't wait to share her plan with Zarina. Less than a minute later, Willow descended the last step into the cavern, finding Zarina grinding something into a powder with one of the pestle and mortar sets.

"I know where they're hiding them."

Zarina looks up from her task, "They're in the house? Please tell me they kept your mother inside her home?"

"I don't know if my mother is there, but the fake Daragis came by wanting to buy more Wolfsbane. When I saw him go inside the church, instead of going back to his antique store, something told me this had everything to do with my parents and nothing with his need to pray. Before I left, I watched as Vicktor and several of the other Gargoyle's forced a chained Troll to open the door under the stairs, where they took several bags I suspect hold the rope coated in Wolfsbane needed to imprison my father."

Zarina nodded her head, "This means he's still alive. I wasn't certain, as Angels are strange creatures and not much is known about them."

"Which is why you can't help me with my stoppage of time."

"Precisely," wiping her hands on a towel beside her.

"When I realized what they were using the Wolfsbane for, I felt sick to my stomach. I'd helped grow miles of that poison for them, all to keep my father held hostage."

Zarina took her face between her warm palms, conveying as much love as she could for the weary young girl. "Don't be saddened by what is in the past. Your father won't place the blame on you, but on Larkin and Opal."

"Maybe so, but I still harbor an immense amount of guilt."

"And perhaps someday soon, you can place that guilt on its rightful owner. Now come on, let's get going, there are people waiting for you."

Moments later, Zarina and Willow stood out front of a much larger bar than Brew Masters. Blood Moon glowed in deep crimson against a black background, dozens of people stood in line as men dressed in suits used wands to scan each eager patron.

"Is this place for humans?" Willow assumed the meeting place would take place in a Faction only venue.

"Humans on the first floor, Faction in the basement, another ruse to hide the singular event when we can all come together as one." Zarina guided her to the back of the building, instructing her where to touch the wall between two glowing lanterns.

Inside, music poured from speakers all around, delivering the sultry voice of an all too familiar song. Willow eyes land on the band as it played intently on stage, Devils Revenge glowing brightly behind them. Glancing around at her fellow patrons, Willow felt significantly under dressed and ducked behind Zarina to change.

"What the—"

"I want to blend in, not stand out like I don't belong here."

Laughing, "Willow, you're half Angel, you will stand out no matter what you wear. But if it makes you feel more comfortable."

Willow pictured an outfit in her mind's eye based on the clothing the women around her are wearing. A short blue dress, open in the back, with a silver chain draped over her right shoulder, helping to hold the dress in place.

Falling in step with the crowd, Willow descended the

metal steps with caution, the beat of the drum matching each step she took. Blue and white lights danced around her in a synchronized performance, reflecting the tempo of the music on stage. There were tall tables covered in black material, a lit candle hovering over the center. U-shaped couches faced the stage, the black leather illuminated from the blue lights blanketing the walls. Trays of colorful drinks moved around the room, floating like the candles, offering thirsty patrons an opportunity to reach out and fill their need.

The man from behind the bar stood at the end of the steps, his hand raised and a smile on his handsome face. "Hello again, Willow. You're looking beautiful as ever."

Zeek possessed the same accent as Lincoln and an equally intimidating in size. "Thank you, Zeek." Placing her hand in his upturned palm. "Pleasure to see you again as well." Willow couldn't get over the difference between the Gargoyle they used to try and trick her and the real werewolf before her. Fake Zeek where the real was kind and clearly a gentleman. Fashionably dressed and easy on the eyes, she liked the real Zeek. The fake one, not so much, with his messy clothing and punk hair.

Zeek let go of Willow's hand the moment her foot hits the floor, knowing the possibility of her mate being in this room was quite high, the last thing he wanted to face is an angry shifter whose mate is being touched without his permission, regardless of the reason. Dipping his head and offering Willow his neck, his movements caught the attention of the shifters in the immediate area who followed suit.

"Why are they doing that?" Willow thought aloud, grateful for the dark room as she could feel the embarrassment heating her neck and chest.

"It's a sign of allegiance. Even though we can no longer communicate mentally, Larkin and his thugs couldn't take away the shifter's basic instincts. Lincoln left instructions on the pledge he gave you. Had you mated last night, I can tell you there would have been a challenge for Alpha, as you, Willow, are stunning."

Zarina reached back, grabbing Willow's hand and pulling her forward. "But there wasn't, so quit making her feel uncomfortable. You know her true mate just might want a piece of you to settle the score."

Zeek lived for moments where he could rile Zarina up, gaining a smile from her while adding a point to his side of the game. "And do we have inside information on who that is?"

Zarina smacked his arm playfully with the back of her hand, a Cheshire grin covering her lips. "No, Zeek. I have my suspicions, same as everyone else. I can't help it if you chose wrong every time. How much did you lose this time?"

"Wait," Willow pulled against Zarina. "You guys bet on who I'd mate with?"

Zeek squared his shoulders, a half grin tugging at his lips.

"My apologies, Willow, we've waited a long time for you to arrive. With our abilities stolen for the past twenty years, we've had to become creative in passing the time."

"Of course," Willow offered, her heart going out to those affected by Larkin and his cruelty. "I can't imagine how hard it's been for you. As I told your brother, I will do everything in my power to make sure you get your abilities back and Larkin severely punished."

Nodding once, Zeek lead them to a table where two men were seated. Both stared at her reverently, standing as Willow approached.

"Gentlemen, this is the woman we've all been waiting for, Willow Morganti. Willow, I present to you, Daragis McCracken of the Irish Dragons and Garath, leader of the Demon Tribe."

Willow shook each man's hand, stunned by the difference in the imposters and the real thing.

"Please, won't you join us?" Garath offered, pulling the chair between them out, assisting Willow as she accepted the seat.

"Damn it!" Zarina shouted, slapping a handful of cash onto the center of the table. "I just knew it would be Garath." Laughter rang out around the table, Zeek's eyes widened in pleasant surprise, tossing his head back in laughter, he too tossed a handful of cash to the center of the table.

"I'm glad you're wrong, Zarina." Turning his pleading

eyes to Willow, "While you are undeniably beautiful, I, like Lincoln, met someone a year before you were born. I can't wait for this to be over so I can return to the Underworld and bring her back here."

Willow caught the sadness in Garath's voice and the glassy appearance filling his dark eyes. Reaching across the table, she lay her hand over his, the birthmark on her wrist pleasantly warm and humming. "I'm so sorry, Garath. I assure you, I am working on a way to break these chains which bind the Factions and return you to your former glory."

Covering her hand with his, "You have the heart of your mother and the fight of your father. I know you will do what you can to help."

The moment was too heavy with raw emotions, with a final squeeze of her hand, Willow shifted her attention to Daragis.

"I must say, Daragis, you are completely different than the individual Larkin tried to pass off as you."

Cracking a smile while raising his drink to his lips, "How so?"

"Well," Willow shifted her position, folding her hands in the center of the table in a neutral position. "For starters, he was nervous and quick tempered, practically demanding an answer if I intended to choose him. Assuring me he would provide me with many children and much wealth."

Daragis leaned over, cocking a single eyebrow. "Tell me Willow, was he as handsome as I am?"

"Fishing for compliments are we, old friend?" A man who Willow recognized as Kieran Priestly, glided over, shaking the hand of each man at the table and placing a kiss to Zarina's cheek before turning his attention to Willow.

"This must be Willow Morganti, the buzz in everyone's conversations." Kieran took the empty seat next to Willow, spinning it around and straddling it. He was sex personified with his wild hair wet with sweat, giving a healthy glow to the skin of his face, and leaving Willow slightly disappointed when the magic of mating didn't occur.

"Pleasure to meet you, Kieran. I'm a huge fan of your music."

"Thank you," Kieran leaned over, placing a kiss to Willow's cheek, the pleasant scent of him encompassing her, filling her with a strange warmth. "I'm a fan of any plan you have to send Larkin to Hell."

Garath adamantly shook his head, "Oh no, don't send him to us. We've had enough of the cheeky bastard."

Willow couldn't help the enormous smile breaking across her face. Even with everything going wrong in their world, these Faction leaders found time to kid around.

"Willow was sharing with us the cock-up job Larkin did trying to replicate us. Making me out to be this greedy bastard who would give her the world as a brood of children."

Taking a deep breath, she readied herself for rejection. "I have a plan, but it will require something I have no right to ask for."

Daragis crossed his massive arms over his chest, leaning back into the leather chair. "Ask away, Willow. If we don't have it, we will find it."

Accustomed to the gruffness of the glamoured Gargoyle who portrayed Daragis, Willow was surprised by the blind generosity of her unspoken request.

"I need a vial of blood," swallowing thickly, setting her gaze on the Dragon who'd exceeded her expectations already. "Your blood to be specific."

Daragis didn't blink an eye as he rolled up his sleeve, exposing his toned arm, "As much as you wish, Willow."

Zarina tapped her fingers on the table, two silver cylinders appearing in her palm. Handing the cylinders to Willow, Daragis used the nail of his pinky to slice through the skin at his wrist, catching the blood in the silver containers. Willow watched with stunned eyes as the thick blood filled the container, while rusty-red in color, its transparent appearance fascinated her.

"What did I miss?" Startled, Willow turned her head in the direction of the new voice at the table, her eyes landing on yet another handsome man with light eyes and long, dark hair. The man gazed back at her, his features full of shock and disbelief. "Holy shit, you look exactly like your mother."

The table fell silent. Zarina took the vials and closed them, sliding them to rest beside Willow's waiting hand. "You will learn to love Azdren and his lack of filter, Willow." She teased, earning a hearty laugh from Azdren.

"I apologize, Willow, I don't mean anything by it. But it's true, you are the splitting image of your mother. As Zarina mentioned, I'm Azdren, leader of the Pride Faction."

"I will take it as a compliment, as I've only seen a few photos of her. It's a pleasure to meet you, Azdren."

The air was once again heavy, something Willow found incredible uncomfortable. Thankfully Garath changes the subject.

"You're just in time, Azdren. Willow here was telling the intriguing story of how Larkin took it upon himself to introduce her to the Factions using poor-quality body doubles."

"Really?"

"Yes and no," Willow clarified. "He managed to parade two into the shop before I suggested meeting the siblings instead." While she felt safe surrounded by the real Faction leaders, she wasn't certain how much of the story she should share with them.

"Dare I ask how they portrayed me?"

"They didn't. Your brother, Tucker, was invited."

"Tucker?" Azdren questioned, a curious tone to his voice. "Now I have to hear the rest of this story."

Garath attempted to conceal his laugh behind a carefully placed hand, while Zarina cleared her throat, a comical look dancing in her eyes.

"Tucker, or the glamoured Gargoyle they used, came late, avoided eye contact and kept to himself. When I asked him a question, he gave the shortest answer possible and returned to his food."

Azdren blinked several times as he stared into Willow's eyes, the hint of a grin slowly creeping on his face. "They made my little brother...shy?"

Willow waited for the punchline to drop from his lips. Snickering broke out all around her as Azdren shook his head before directing her attention to a handsome man sitting at a table full of shifters, his animated movements and huge smile made it clear he was the center of attention. "That's Tucker. Never met a stranger and it's guaranteed if he's invited to a party, it will be one hell of a time."

Where the glamoured Gargoyle was reserved, dressed in clothing he clearly felt uncomfortable in, the real Tucker was full of life, dressed in a pressed shirt with the first few buttons undone, a gold chain hanging from his neck and disappearing behind the material of the shirt.

"I don't get it." Garath thought aloud, pulling Willow's attention back to the table. "Why the need to fake the Faction leaders, making them into something completely the opposite of who they really are."

"Two reasons," Daragis added, leaning on his elbows, the

cut to his arm completely healed, not even a red area remaining where he'd cut his skin. "Larkin needs Willow to choose him as her mate in order to steal her power. He can't risk her meeting the real Faction leaders and mating with one of us. So, he took the worst qualities a human can have, something he could obtain by reading any number of books or magazines, and gave each of those Gargoyles a handful of them. Guaranteeing our Willow will settle for the lesser of the evils, himself."

Sadly, Daragis was right, that is exactly what Willow had done…settled.

"What he didn't count on, was the beautiful woman also having a brilliant mind, and the ablility to see past his façade and find the truth."

Willow wished she could agree with him, take credit for out-smarting Larkin. The sad truth was it had all been a matter of luck, being in the right place at the right time and eavesdropping on a conversation not meant for her.

"Which is why I know whatever plan she has swimming around in her head, I will do anything I can to help her make it happen." Tapping his index finger on the table beside Willow's hand, the thump competing with the base of the music pumping overhead. "If you need more blood, I'm in my shop not far from here, next to Priestly's Collectables."

Willow was surprised by his admission as she understood none of the Factions could do business in the Quarter. "You own a shop in the Quarter?"

"I own a shop in the Quarter."

"Mathias," Daragis announced in a surprised, yet happy tone. "I was beginning to think you weren't going to make an appearance tonight." Rising from his chair, Daragis extended a hand across the table as Willow turned her attention to the new arrival.

The smell of leather and something uniquely sweet washed over her, a low hum prickling her birthmark. The sensation was instantly addicting and like nothing she'd ever felt before. As her eyes landed on the dark leather of an overcoat to her right, the defining sound of her heartbeat pounded in her ears. Willow's breath caught in her throat as her eyes glided up the leather, caressing over a fitted black shirt, lingering on the defined chin decorated with well-groom facial hair. Dark hair, short on the sides in a perfect quaff, frame the man's face. But it's his eyes, the indescribable blue from her dreams, the ones matching the raven's.

The room disappeared, the Faction leaders and the battle with the Gargoyles forgotten the moment his gaze locked with hers. Thousands of tiny ribbons pulled them together, fusing her to him in a bond even death couldn't sever.

Mathias had her in his arms before another breath could leave his lungs, her chair clambering to floor behind them. His mouth, acting of its own accord, covered her delicate lips with his, this intense need to touch her all-consuming.

A warm sensation filled her as his tongue swept across her

lips, demanding entrance as his grip on her back and waist tightened. Mathias's chest vibrated under her fingers, a deep growl as if an animal warning their prey of an approaching attack filled the tiny space between them. Willow welcomed it, basking in the heat of it, somehow knowing this sound was something only she could pull from him. Mathias was a skilled kisser, so much more than any other man she'd kissed. But as the purring continued and he dominated her mouth, flashes of places she's never visited appeared in her mind.

A woman, dressed in a long skirt, her hair tied behind her head, several tendrils sticking to her sweat-slick face. Her smile was warm despite the tired and dirty features of her face. It's clear the woman is not from this time, as told by her clothing. The scene around the woman is of an ancient village, but before Willow can scan the scene, a dark horse galloped at full speed down the dirt path behind the woman, swinging what looks to be a sword, severing the woman's head from her shoulders.

Mathias pulled her tighter, turning his head to a different angle, sliding his leg between hers, fueling the fire already burning hot inside her.

The picture shifted to what looked to be an ancient church, a priest standing on the stone steps, his hands raised as if trying to gain the attention of a crowd. Several men stood off to the right, their skin pale and clothing black and weathered. One of the men points at something in the crowd, the priest shook his head adamantly before dropping to his knees, pleading with the man. Horses, much like the previous scene, galloped at top speed, blocking her view of the men on the steps. When the last horse raced by and with the dust swirling in the light from a nearby fire, Willow watched as one of the men who stood off in the corner, had the priest practically bent in half, his face buried in the crook of his neck. Seconds before Willow's view changed again, the man tossed the priest limp and lifeless body to the steps of the church, blood dripping down his chin.

Willow's heart began to race when the picture flashed to a room full of couples in various sex acts, a few enjoying more than one partner. Blue lights from overhead blanketed the naked bodies, making the shadows appear more pronounced, gratefully hiding some of the more risqué events from Willow's eyes. Confusion wrapped its ugly head around her, filling her mind with questions as to why these pictures are pulling her attention away from devouring Mathias. It wasn't until the reflection from a mirrored wall showed her the man she's currently wrapped around staring back at her that she realized these were his memories. Unable to close her mind's eye, she watched in horror as at least five beautiful women surround Mathias, kissing and slowly removing his clothing before taking turns allowing him to feed from them, and then surrendering themselves to him sexually. Willow could feel the pleasurable sensation Mathias felt as the rich blood ran down his throat, her body vibrated with the pleasure he received at the hands and bodies of the women surrounding him.

Unable to stomach anymore, Willow pushed at Mathias's chest, struggling to sever the connection and rid her of the heart-wrenching scene in her mind.

Mathias allowed her to break the kiss, dropping his hands

from around her. He'd seen the way her dress barely covered her body the minute he'd walked into the room, the essence of her calling to his soul. Kissing her was everything, more addicting than the richest blood he'd ever sampled, more precious than any jewel hidden in his safe across town. Shrugging off his jacket, he held her gaze as he draped it around her shoulders, covering what was his.

"I don't share, Willow. Not even with an innocent gaze by an appreciative eye." Pulling the lapels of the jacket closed, and tugging her back to his chest, "You, Willow Morganti, are mine."

Willow struggled to catch her breath and clear her mind, trying desperately to separate the man in her head from the one pulling her to his chest.

"That's not entirely true." Willow said with conviction, stopping his progression, her eyes finding his blue ones.

Never in Mathias's three-hundred plus years had he ever regretted spending time in the company of one of his feeders, drinking from them until he quenched his thirst, then sampling their offerings for relieving his sexual cravings. He never cared if he left a woman with hurt feelings on the rare occasion he entered into a relationship with a human, not bothering to glamour them into forgetting him. He basked in the reputation he'd acquired, making him a topic of conversation among the other Factions. Until now that is. He'd been cautioned by his previous alpha, the man responsible for changing him at an early age, that his whole life would playout like a movie on the big screen for his one true mate, another level in the gods twisted sense of humor.

"I apologize for anything you saw causing you displeasure."

Mathias looked down into the eyes of his perfect match, feeling her pulling away fracturing a piece of his dead heart. The bitterness of her pain swirled inside his mouth, making him sick with disgust for making her unhappy.

"Your eyes," Willow searched his face, the women from his past momentarily forgotten. "You were in my dreams. I couldn't see your face, but your eyes."

"I know," Mathias lowered his lips to hers, closing his eyes and sending a word of thanks this beautiful creature was his.

"I prayed you were real and not a side effect of Larkin's treachery." Cupping his face between her palms. "Are you real?"

"I am now, Willow. For the first time in my dark life, I'm real."

Willow understood what Zarina meant when she spoke of the need to be with him. She wanted him, wanted to give him the gift of her virginity.

"Soon, my love."

Embarrassed, Willow tried to hide her face. "Did I say that out loud?"

Tucking his finger under her chin, pulling her eyes back to his. "No, it's one of the many perks of finding one's other half."

"You can hear my thoughts?"

Nodding, "And you mine, Beauteous."

Surprise colored Willow's face, "Oh my, God! It was you; the note, the handkerchief, the rose."

Unable to stop himself, the relief and happiness wrapped around her words reached that place in his soul he didn't know existed, the need to kiss her too great to ignore.

"Yes, Luprin, the raven, has helped my me and my family since we were chased into the sewers. He called Lincoln, but unfortunately, they were too late. You cannot imagine how difficult it is knowing you're inside the house where we celebrated your parent's union and I had to wait until tonight to see you, hold you, hoping beyond measure you'd finally sought out Zarina so she could get you here."

"You have no idea how many nights I sat on the balcony talking to Luprin as if he could understand me."

"Oh, he does. And while he succeeded in bringing your voice to me, he failed at describing how captivatingly gorgeous you are."

"In your note, you called me Beauteous. Why not my name?"

"Because that's what my father called my mother until the day she died."

"The woman in your memory."

Mathias nodded his head, not ready to divulge the story of how much his life changed the day she died, and he and his brother were taken prisoner by a bunch of rogue vampires.

"She was the love of his life and he sacrificed everything to be with her."

Willow sensed the moment was a heavy burden for him, despite the leather and bad ass image he projected, Mathias had a soft layer. One where he kept the good memories of those he loved.

"You know, Luprin could have lied to you, told you I was pretty and in reality, I looked like Saige or Brynn without their glamour." Willow teased, nipping at his bottom lip, coaching another purr from his chest.

"Not possible. The gods would never give me someone who wasn't everything my heart desired." Mathias believed this from the moment he stood before his coven and pledged to be the leader they deserved. Accepting all of requirements he must fulfil, including taking on a mate if the gods so chose.

"I don't know about the rest of you gentleman, but I would hate to be in Mathias's shoes. Newly mated, but unable to seal the bond for what," Zeek raised his watch free arm, pretending to gaze at the time. "Too many days."

Keeping Willow close, "Careful, Zeek. I still owe you an ass kicking for touching Willow earlier."

Zeek shot Mathias a cocky smirk, "We can step outside. Although that would waste precious time with your new mate."

Using the edge of his boot, Mathias righted Willow's vacated chair, sliding fluidly into the leather seat and pulling her to sit on his lap.

"You have to go back, don't you?" Willow's voice sounded so broken, shattering the majority of Mathias's resolve.

"Not yet, and not like before."

"How so?"

"Our bonding gave me a little of your magic, I can feel it coursing through me."

"What does that mean for you?"

"Besides having a part of you with me, we will have to wait and see as I've never mated before. Angels are a mystery, even to someone as old as myself or Zarina."

"Will I still see you in my dreams?"

"If I have anything to do with it, you'll do more than see me."

Willow felt as if every eye in the room was upon her, scrutinizing everything from her swollen lips to the black leather duster covering her dress and exposed skin. Sweeping her gaze across the room, dancing from one table to the next as Daragis bragged to Mathias of the brilliant plan she'd be about to share with them. Mathias responded with a squeeze to her waist and a boasting of confidence his mate was of course brilliant. Where she assumed judgement would greet her, the opposite was true, the majority of the patrons around her carried on with the joviality of the evening, ignoring the blatant display being carried out. Perhaps they expected this of Mathias, assuming she would be another notch in his bedpost.

Willow's throat grew thick, her breathing pausing when her eyes landed across the aisle on Kieran and the two women in his company. The first, a beautiful redhead perched on the back of the sofa, her legs spread wide as Kieran drank from her inner thigh. The second, a darkhaired woman, naked as the day she was born, her face hidden from Willow's view as she bobbed her head up and down, across Kieran's lap giving him a blow job.

Raising to her feet, the image of Mathias indulging in the same activity flooded her mind, making her blood boil with anger, while yet an incredible amount of sadness washed over her. Feeling as if being torn in two, half of her wanting to claim Mathias here and now, while the other wanted to run from this bar and back to the comforts of her childhood room in Florida.

Shrugging out of his coat, Willow dropped the spell hiding her borrowed jeans and t-shirt, no longer feeling the need to blend into the crowd.

"Beauteous?" Mathias called to her, after his coat fell like a weight into his lap. He could feel the confliction inside of her, see the retreat in her eyes. It's clear something, or someone, had upset her, and whoever was responsible was about to die.

"I'm fine, Mr. Priestly." Willow moved to stand beside Zarina, the most she could do to satisfy her need to run at the moment.

"Mr. Priestly? I don't think so." Mathias barked out, allowing his need for her to take over. Tossing his coat to the table, the force shattering glass and sending his fellow Faction leaders to their feet, a grumble to their lips. Movement to the side gained a slice of his attention, several of his regular feeders approached, oblivious to his partially mated status.

"Kieran, take my feeders to the bac—"

"Take care of your harem yourself." Willow interrupted, venom strangling each word. Mathias was equally turned on and pissed off, momentarily forgetting her ability to hear his thoughts. Unwilling to allow Willow to see him as anything less than a devoted mate, Mathias tossed her over his shoulder, darting the both of them across the room and out the back before a gasp could reach Willow's lips. Placing her back on her feet, Mathias sandwiched her against the wall, his hands cracking the brick on either side of her head from the force of his momentum.

"I do not have a *harem*," Mathias placed emphasis on the Willow's choice of words, the bite to his words causing her to flinch. "Those women, the ones both in my memory and in the room back there, are members of my coven. Their sole purpose is to feed me, their leader."

"And have sex," Willow tossed back, refusing to stand idle as this man used his size and speed advantage over her.

"Yes, Willow. I've had sex with several of them, something both of us wanted at the time."

Willow felt suddenly cheated, having saved her virginity for some unknown reason while the man she was destined to spend forever with had tossed his away like an empty soda can.

"You know, Beauteous," Mathias lowered his lips to the shell of her ear, the vibrating sensation wreaking havoc on her core. "This is going to develop into one hell of a tale we will share with our children when they are older. How their father was an idiot and nearly lost the only woman he would ever love."

Despite the fire building inside of her, Mathias could feel Willow pulling away, slowing shutting her thoughts off to him, something he couldn't allow to happen. Covering her lips with his, using every inch of his body touching hers to push home how much she meant to him. Their time together was growing short, his need to feed would have to wait until he returned to his prison under the city. Palming her face, he tried to kiss away the thought of her going back to the house covered in lies and deception. Mathias could smell Larkin on her the moment he first kissed her and wanted nothing more than to bathe her in his scent, casting away the stench of the glamoured Gargoyle. But he couldn't, for as much as he could smell Larkin, the opposite would be true, jeopardizing the plan he'd heard about.

Pulling back, Mathias rested his forehead against hers, he could hear his coven grumble their displeasure about the time and how the sun would be rising in a couple of hours. "Avoid contact with anyone when you return to the house, until after you shower. Get rid of these clothes so they can't smell me on you."

Willow nodded her head in understanding, keeping her head down, she pushed passed Mathias before she could talk herself out of it. Following the sound of the music, she found the table and a worried looking Zarina. Biding goodbye to the Faction leaders, Willow motioned to the door, not bothering to check over her shoulder to say a final goodbye to Mathias.

As the pale colors of a new day began filling her room, Willow tucked into her blankets, a single tear trickling down her face, a result of the sensation she felt covering her, one she recalled from the brief time she'd spent in Mathias's memories. Somewhere under the city, the man the gods chose for her was having sex with at least one gorgeous woman, and it certainly wasn't her.

CHAPTER TWO

"I found it!" Willow cried victoriously, holding up the orange spell book in her right hand as she walked into the library. She suspected she'd interrupted a moment between Larkin and Brynn given the way he turned his back to her, hiding what Willow imagined was the impossible erection.

"It's going to take a lot of work, and perhaps all the power you and Saige have, but I've got it."

Brynn pushed passed a still cowering Larkin, making her way around the large table, her eyes fixed on the book in Willow's hand. "Where in the world did you find this?"

Holding back a laugh, Willow watched in amusement as Brynn stood with her mouth agape in disbelief, her eyes fixed on the book clasped securely in her fingers.

"In the solarium behind one of the rose bushes. I was trimming them back when I noticed the corner sticking out." Willow lied. How the ease of doing so had changed since coming here, apparently, she was becoming a product of her environment. "My mother must have stowed it away before she was killed." Adding the latter as bait to see if Brynn would take it.

"Were there anymore?" Brynn questioned, reaching out for the book, unknowingly falling into the trap Willow laid out for her.

"Not that I could find, but we don't need any others. This has the spell we're looking for." Willow shook the book for emphasis, shifting her focus to Larkin, who thankfully had collected himself.

"I can save you; we can save you." Willow held her hand out for Larkin, harnessing the pain she felt from Mathias's activities earlier, grateful for the emotional crack in her voice and the well of tears filling her lower lids to add a layer to her deception.

"We don't have much time, Willow. The blood moon is almost here." Brynn added, her eyes still glued to the spellbook Willow created before getting out of bed, using the spell as a warmup to dissolve the connection with Mathias. She didn't know how, or if it was even possible, but she refused to spend another day able to feel him that way.

Larkin followed the same path as Brynn, coming to stand before Willow, locking his gaze on her. Raising his hands, he framed her face with the palm of his hands, using the pads of his thumbs to wipe away the lines left behind on her tear stained cheeks. She smelled different to him today, something spicy with a hint of rotten earth. While the scent was familiar, he didn't have time to care, and chose to assume it was the result of digging around in those dead rose bushes her bitch of a mother loved so much.

"If this is true, we don't have to wait for the ball, Willow. End the spell and claim me as your mate." Larkin could feel the energy washing off of her, his plan to this point had worked better than he'd hoped. Time, however, was not on his side. Based on how frail Cerise looked last night, it wouldn't be long before she finally died, leaving all her magic to the wretched human under his hands. He needed her virginity and, by extension, all the power pulsing inside her veins once she chose him and he strangled the life from her and ultimately the other Factions.

"As wonderful as that sounds," Willow whispered, slowly opening and closing her eyes in a bashful manner. "I want to follow the rules, making the announcement before the other Factions."

She knew she need to keep him hanging for as long as possible if her plan was to work. And it would. Her parents and the other Factions needed her to pull this off, which is what gave her the needed courage to push up on her tiptoes and place a gentle kiss to the side of Larkin's grotesque lips.

"As long as you choose me, I don't care how we do it." It was lie, Larkin wanted nothing more than to spin Willow around, rip the clothes from her body and fuck her hard against the table beside them, watching the life fall from her eyes as her magic filled his body.

"Good, because I need you to help most of all." Pushing passed him, unable to hold her breath a second longer. In the days since she'd quit drinking the tea, the smells in the house had changed nearly as fast as the appearance. Larkin's being the most offensive.

"Really?"

"Yes, I need to speak with Daragis."

"Why?" Of all the Factions, Daragis was the most difficult for Larkin to mimic as he spent the least amount of time in the Quarter. Most of the information he'd obtained was from memory and he'd already screwed up once, telling Martise, the Gargoyle Ophelia glamoured to look like Daragis, that he was originally from Bolivia, not Ireland where his lair remained protected. Lucky for them, Willow wasn't smart enough to catch the error.

"Because according to the spell, we need Dragon's blood."

Willow laid the book on the table, standing back with her arms crossed as Brynn reached out for the leather-bound pages as if a child with a new toy, flipping it open to the page she'd marked with ribbon. A satisfied smile washed over her lips as Larkin placed a loving hand in the middle of Brynn's back, his body naturally molding to hers in a lover's stance. Willow took pause as she observed Brynn's boney finger scanning the letters on the aged parchment, as Larkin's talons moved lovingly up and down in what she assumed was comfort. Larkin may not care for her, but he truly loved Brynn.

"I expect him to be here at any moment to collect more Wolfsbane. I'd like you to be in the room when I ask him for the gift he promised me."

Larkin dropped his hand from Brynn, rounding the corner to stand beside Willow. "But you said you were choosing me."

Willow placed her hand on his chest, the scars marring his skin felt odd to her, as if filled with magic. A familiar growl echoed in her head, instantly irritating her as she knew immediately who the owner of the snarl belonged to. *"You're killing me, Beauteous."*

Picturing Mathias standing in a doorway in her head, she mentally shut the door, effectively closing the link between them.

"Larkin, we need his blood, that is all." Tapping her fingers three times before drifting them across his chest and arm, sending him a wink before returning to the spellbook.

WILLOW GLANCED AT THE CLOCK ON THE FAR WALL AS THE door to the shop opened and the fake Daragis stepped over the threshold, entering the store at roughly the same time as his previous visits. She noticed Saige, for whatever reason, was skittish as he crossed the room, leaning his beefy arm against the glass of the counter.

"Daragis," she called in a voice so sweet she worried she

might develop a cavity from it. "Do you have a moment to speak with me?"

Daragis glanced between Larkin and Brynn, Willow assumed waiting for permission or an escape route. She ignored the slight nod Larkin shot him, follow by the foreign words spoken in what she suspected was clipped, based on his tone.

"Of course, Willow. Anything for you."

Separating the distance between them, sending Larkin a covert wink as she took the final steps. Mimicking Daragis position, "The last time we spoke, you mentioned something about a gift for me. Now, I may not know much about mythical creatures, but I do know Dragons are known for keeping their word." Willow borrowed the latter from the real Daragis and the way he'd pledged his alliance to her.

"I'd like to collect that gift, see for myself if you really can give me all those children you promised me." Wiggling her eyebrows for emphasis, nearly losing her composure when the fake Daragis began coughing in surprise.

"Certainly, I can bring back the paperclip you chose—"

"I have no need for paperclips, Daragis." Willow interrupted, flirting tossed to the side and a much more serious tone reflecting in her voice. "Brynn and I have discovered a spell which will tell me exactly how worthy you are of my choice. The spell requires a sample of your blood.

Which is what I ask of you in way of the gift you swore to me."

Daragis grumbled something under his breath as he reluctantly shed his suit jacket, rolling up the sleeve on his right arm, and exposing the skin there. Unlike the real Daragis, this dressed up Gargoyle had crocodile tears in his eyes when Saige laid out the supplies to capture the blood. The fear in his eyes growing by leaps and bounds when Brynn moved the shiny knife in her hand toward him.

"Allow me," Willow stopped her, sharing a look which couldn't be misunderstood. "It is my gift, after all."

Brynn handed the knife to Willow, nodding with a polite smile on her face, taking a step back and closer to Larkin. The longer Willow remained in their presence, the more she noticed the attraction between them. Had it always been this obvious? Or had Ophelia's tea been that potent? She decided it didn't really matter, getting on with her plan did.

Gripping the handle of the knife, Willow recalled how Daragis made a vertical cut in the skin of his forearm. Attempting to repeat the cut, she's met with resistance. No matter how hard she pushed, the blade refused to pierce the skin.

"You have some thick skin there, Mr. McCracken."

When her comment is met with silence, she glanced from the blade of the knife to the face of the imposter, finding his eyes clenched tight and his head turned away as if unable to see his own blood. Hiding her amusement, Willow lowered her head, taking another stab with the knife, only to have the same result.

Larkin moved forward, placing his hand over Willow's, "Here, allow me to help." Pushing the tip of the blade through the skin with ease, a stream of gargoyle blood dripped into the wooden bowl below.

"Thank you," Willow said automatically. Just as lies were a big part of the people surrounding her, being polite was ingrained in her.

"Of course, it benefits us both." Larkin added, returning the wink from earlier.

Willow returned her gaze to the blood flowing freely into the bowl. Had she not seen first-hand what Dragon blood truly looked like, she would be more amazed than disgusted at the black sludge pooling in the bottom of the wooden bowl. The putrid smell hit her nose, a combination of low tide and wet dog, forcing her to breathe through her mouth.

"I believe we have more than enough." Saige announced when the level in the bowl came up halfway. The fake Daragis released a breath, his massive shoulders slumping in relief as he jerked his still bleeding arm back.

"Yes, thank you, Daragis." Willow handed the knife to Larkin, wiping her hands on her apron, the feel of Larkin's skin giving her the creeps. Eyeing the box, she'd packed earlier, Willow crossed the room, hoisting the heavy crate from the shelf. "I was hoping you would agree to my request," her words reflected her struggle to maintain the weight of the box. Daragis noticed her difficulty, forgetting his ailing arm, he took several measured steps, lifting the crate with ease from her hands. "Thank you, Daragis. I put in a few extra bottles in there, no charge this time." Willow hoped this imposter would keep in character of the role he was playing, Dragons may be keepers of their word, but they are thieves at heart, stealing treasures for their collection.

Not bothering to bid anyone a goodbye, the fake Daragis looked to the contents of the box and then scurried out of the shop and onto the sidewalk. His heavy gait moved him out of Willow's sight and down the block before she could blink.

Turning to Saige, "Bottle that blood up good and tight, we can't afford to waste a single drop."

CHAPTER THREE

Hours after the shop closed and the music from the streets filled the house, Willow found herself tucked away in her favorite hiding place. When the grandfather clock in the hall began chiming its announcement of midnights arrival, she watched as once again a Troll was pushed and prodded down the hall, its cries of protest silenced by what Willow assumed was another spell. The shackles on his feet and hands digging into its flesh, creating deep gashes which made her incredibly angry. She silently vowed to make certain the Troll was allowed to choose the Gargoyles punishment for such cruel treatment.

Despite having witnessed this before, Willow clenched her fists when the Gargoyle took his spear, stabbing it repeatedly into the back of the Troll, demanding the poor thing open the door. Willow's anger turned to pride when after several minutes and hundreds of jabs, the Troll stood motionless in the hall as if refusing to help them, even if it meant its demise. As she prepared to create a distraction, giving them reason to take the Troll away so she wouldn't see it, Larkin came trudging around the corner. Pushing everyone, including the Troll out of the way, he tapped his hand on the wall in sequence, the contact creating glowing shapes which appear on the wall and allowing the door to swing open.

Willow closed her eyes and thought back to the day the fake Lincoln made her angry and then to the night she caught Larkin and Brynn together allowing those hurt feelings to do their magic. Testing the waters, Willow allowed one of her eyes to open, jumping to her feet and racing down the steps when she found everyone still as statues. The pendulum of the grandfather clock was suspended in mid-swing, as was Larkin with his hand raised and wings pointed to the ceiling.

Skirting around the lot, Willow took one final glance at the Troll before stepping into complete darkness. Based on the previous occasions she'd accidently stopped time; she knew her window of opportunity was limited. Using capture as inspiration, she ignored the cobwebs and dirt, concentrating instead on landing her foot on the next step and not falling into the pitch-black sea of the unknown. With her focus so intense, she was startled and nearly lost her footing when a deep voice echoed in her head.

"Beauteous?"

Gripping the edge of the brick wall, she took a moment to balance herself, tapped down her racing heart and listened for any movement from behind her. When all she could hear was her heart pounding in her ears and a dripping sound below her, she began her descent, once again ignoring Mathias and his persistence for the time being. Willow counted twenty-seven steps before the warm glow of light in the distance reached her, quickening her steps as the hum of magic grew more intense around her.

Willow imagined if her parents were being held prisoner down here, the chance of more Gargoyles guarding them was fairly certain. It was with this in mind she kept her movements quiet and her body as close to the wall as possible. When her foot landed on the final step, the light from a lantern hanging from a hook on the wall cast enough illumination for her to see there were no guards. Only one long room with two iron cages separated by a pile of discarded rope stacked high on a wooden table.

In the cell to her left, a dark-haired man sat resting his head against the brick wall, his hands and feet bound with layers of blue stained rope. His hair much longer than in the photo in her mother's room, his muscular physique still present despite his years of confinement. However, Willow would recognize him anywhere.

"Dad?" Willow whispered, taking a final look back up the long steps before running across the room, wrapping her fingers around the iron bars.

Orifiel's head shot up, his eyes locking on the beautiful woman staring back at him, her features an exact match for his wife who lay dying just beyond the table. Shifting his gaze to her right wrist, he remained silent, waiting for her to turn her arm so he could catch a glimpse of the flesh of her wrist. Over the years Larkin sent a number of charmed Gargoyles made to look like his what his daughter should have, had she survived. Each failed to bear his mark, a gift he gave his daughter before she was ripped from his arms. He watched as thousands of emotions flashed across the woman's delicate features, each one a carbon copy of the woman who stole his heart all those years ago.

Choosing to remain silent, unwilling to give the guards who were due to arrive any minute another laugh at his expense in believing the prior imposters really were his beloved daughter. Instead he shifted his feet from the bed, the blisters covering his skin from the Wolfsbane reminding him of his lack of power. As he moved his hands to rest in his lap, he caught movement from the corner of his eye, stealing his attention and increasing the rhythm of his heartbeat.

He'd hoped this day would come and yet feared it just as much. Darting his head in the direction of the young woman as she slammed an open hand against the metal bars, he sees it, the mark he placed on the wrist of his infant daughter. Cautiously, Orifiel scooted to the end of the cot, the rope digging into his skin, opening the healing wounds from years of continuous abuse. Rising to his feet, he shifted the short distance between himself and the young lady, purposely exposing her to the blue rope around his wrists.

"Touch the rope." He demanded, needing to believe the mark was real and not another illusion created by Larkin and his sidekicks.

Willow blinked rapidly, hearing the sound of her father's voice for the first time, its deep base sending a warm sensation down her back and around her heart like a vine in early spring. Glancing down at his wrists, she cringed at the blisters and open wounds, the need to do something to help him almost too much to ignore.

"Touch the rope or get out of here." Willow jerked at the harshness of his demand, shoving her hand through the narrow bars, sucking air through her teeth as the mark on her wrist screamed in pain.

Orifiel stood torn in half as he watched the young girl grimace in pain, the need to protect her stronger than his need to be certain this wasn't another trick. He could feel his magic pulsing inside of her, as if seeing an old friend, he'd lost touch with.

Joy trumped the pain in her wrist as she locked eyes with her father. Recognition reflecting back at her. Willow let go of the rope, taking her father's hand in hers, a blue glow shown around them the moment she wrapped her fingers with his, sending a strange tingle through her body.

"It's you. Willow, you're here."

Orifiel prayed to every god he knew this day would come and yet feared it just as much. He could feel his magic beg to return to him, feel it move from her body to his filling him with an intensity he hadn't felt for twenty years.

"I am, Dad. I had to warn you."

Orifiel pulled his daughter closer, doing his best to avoid touching her skin with the rope. "Warn me of what?"

Willow told her father of the switch she'd made with the Wolfsbane and rose. How she continued to make Larkin believe she'd chosen him, all the while searching for where he'd hidden them.

"Have you chosen a mate?" Orifiel regretted how much of his daughter's life he'd missed. He would spend eternity making up for it, starting with making certain the Faction leader she'd chosen understood his expectations.

Willow dropped her eyes, finding the blue rope secured around her father's wrists enough of a distraction to avoid the unpleasant conversation. "I met with the leaders…" She drifted off, hoping he wouldn't press for more.

Orifiel dipped his head down in order to gain her attention, sharing a smile he hoped would put her at ease. "And…"

Willow stood up straight, swallowing back the hurt she felt at Mathias's decision to have sex with his feeder despite their connection.

"And it doesn't matter, Dad. Once I found out I don't have to mate in order to stay alive after my birthday, I'm not so sure I want to tie myself down to any of the Factions. At least not now."

As an Angel, Orifiel had the ability to tell when a human or Faction was lying, and right now, his beautiful daughter was trying desperately to separate herself from a deep wound created by one of the men he considered his friends. Bending over, he used the guise of kissing the back of her hand, taking in a healthy lung-full of her scent to gain the knowledge of which one of them he was either defending or separating their head from their body. Each Faction had a distinct fragrance to him; the Dragons carried an essence of roasted coffee, Werewolves a blend of blueberries and chocolate, and the Prides smelled of various spices, ranging from vanilla with the Panthers to cinnamon with the Mountain Lions. His least favorite was the rotting dirt smell of the Fairies. The Witches were undoubtedly his favorite, recalling how many mornings he woke wrapped around his wife the smell of lemon and lavender invading his senses. And while those two scents were there, the lingering scent of cloves hung in the background, telling him more than his upset daughter could.

"Mathias is a good man, Willow. Mind telling your poor, old father what my friend did to upset you?"

Willow looked at her father through confused eyes. She'd struggled to keep her emotions in check, banking on the fact the man before her knew nothing about her.

Orifiel recalled the same look on Cerise's face the first time he'd been able to get beyond her carefully constructed wall of everything is fine, when in fact she was struggling to understand something he'd said to her. While the comment on his part was innocent, to the woman he loved it was the tallest mountain she'd ever considered climbing and, just as the product of their love who stood before him felt it easier to take another path which would lead her to a world of heartache, it was his job to get to the bottom of it and make her see the truth.

Willow wasn't certain how her father knew it was Mathias who'd left a bad taste in her mouth. For the briefest of moments, she considered telling him what she needed to and then going back upstairs, filling the night with meaningless tasks to avoid falling asleep and dreaming of Mathias. Something told her the effort would be in vain as clearly he'd been able to see through her. With a heavy sigh and her eyes focused on the cobwebs above her head, Willow told her father everything she'd experienced since her car breaking down on the highway.

"Tell me, sweetheart. When you used your abilities upstairs to halt time, did you picture Mathias or Larkin?"

Orifiel was all too aware of the fine line between love and hate. The dimensions so much thinner when a Faction mating bond was involved. He thought to his own dilemma when he fell hard and fast for Cerise and the many obstacles which stood in their way. He hoped his intervention would save Willow and Mathias precious time and heartache.

"Larkin, why?"

"Interesting," he baited, the flash in her eyes told him he was right.

"Did I do something wrong? I can't control anything and Zarina can't help me, says she knows next to nothing of

Angels and our magic..." Willow trailed off, her mind in overdrive, worried she'd said too much, yet not enough.

"Your mother is a rambler too, especially when she is overwhelmed." Tugging at Willow's fingers, wishing he could wrap his arms around her and take away the confusion inside her head. "Larkin was correct when he said Faction men, especially vampires, are sexual creatures."

Willow opened her mouth to speak, but Orifiel squeezed her digits tighter. "Willow, before you get upset again, let me see if I can show you what really happened."

Acting before his daughter could argue, Orifiel closed his eyes, using their connected hands to fuel his gift. Like pictures from a photo album, he shuffled through the last few days until he landed on Willow sitting at a table with the Faction leaders surrounding her. Orifiel paused for a moment, taking a hard look at the faces of friends he hadn't seen in twenty years. He couldn't wait for this imprisonment to be over, having his wife once again beside him and the Factions living in harmony as reflected in the smiles around the table.

Shuffling through several more minutes, Orifiel stops when his eyes fall on the sad and slightly pissed off face of his daughter as she leaves the bar. Allowing the scene to fall around them, "Dad, please, I don't want to see Mathias having sex."

Orifiel shifted his gaze to Willow, the sadness in her eyes enough to bring him to his knees. Tucking a piece of fallen hair behind her ear, "Sweetheart, I didn't bring you here to watch a couple engage in sex. I brought you here to see what really happened after you left. If what you think is true, then you have every reason to deny the mating. But if it's not…" Leaving his statement open, he motioned in the direction where Mathias stood, a haunted look upon his face. "You know, Willow, for a man about to engage in sex, he looks almost grief-stricken."

Willow refused to agree with her father, choosing instead to allow this to play out until the moment where Mathias and his whorish ways proved her point. Her father hadn't been there when the feelings washed over her, hadn't been forced to avoid sleep for the past few days in order to keep from seeing the man who, just like the others, had betrayed her.

Orifiel was no stranger to Mathias and his taste in women, having the need to sample as many as inhumanly possible. There was a time, although brief, where he envied him, lived vicariously through the lavish parties he and his brother Kieran threw. However, the second he heard his sweet Cerise's voice, his envy turned to pity as he knew Mathias wasn't really sampling. He was searching for the one true woman to fill the emptiness in his heart. By the look on his face, Mathias had found her in his daughter, and it was killing him to let her go.

Willow held tight to her father's hand as Mathias turned with his head hung low and headed for the door. A burn filled her chest at the sadness she felt coming off Mathias as he, like her father stated, looked grief-stricken. The two women who'd been feeding Kieran followed behind him at a respectful distance as the remaining patrons inside the bar drifted toward the exit.

Orifiel raised his hand and pushed time forward a few minutes, finding Mathias in a candle lit room he didn't recognize. The Priestly's, like the other Factions, surrounded themselves in luxury, owning homes and business around the globe. Anger brewed in his chest as he perused his friend's surroundings. This was Larkin's doing, reducing the Faction leaders to fragments of themselves. Refusing to allow his anger to overshadow the reason he was here, Orifiel pushed time forward once more, landing on Mathias as he stood with his feeders, the moment that would make or break the bond.

No matter how much she wanted to, Willow couldn't pull her eyes from Mathias and the deplorable conditions he lived in, or the two beautiful women who stood before him.

"She is beautiful, sir." The red-haired woman spoke, extending her arm in Mathias's direction. *"Your children will be the envy of Coven."*

Mathias shook his head, reaching for a bottle sitting on an upturned crate, raising it to his lips and draining the contents.

"She's the most beautiful woman I've ever seen." Mathias says, his eyes fixed off in the distance as he handed the empty bottle to the woman. *"But she's up there with Larkin, while I'm stuck down here in this hell and there isn't a goddamn thing I can do about it."*

As the red-haired woman took the bottle, the dark-haired woman stepped closer, *"Please calm yourself, sir. Willow is a Morganti Witch, she would never—"*

"I'm well aware of who she is!" Mathias roared, forcing the young woman to drop her head and take a step back. *"But that bastard has touched her, put his disgusting hands and mouth where he had no right."*

Mathias speared his fingers into the hair at the top of his head, sitting with a huff in a chair that had seen much better days. The red-haired woman appeared beside him, nudging his shoulder with the bottle he'd handed her earlier. Mathias dropped his hands but shook his head when she offered the bottle.

"Starving yourself won't get this over with any faster, sir."

Mathias looked to the woman, nodded his head and took the offered bottle.

"I'll let the other feeders know to collect their blood and have it sent to you."

Mathias tipped the bottle back, his eyes closing in ecstasy as a single drop of crimson escaped his lips.

"You see, Willow, vampires are passionate creatures, especially when it comes to their mates. Mathias wasn't having sex when you felt the sensation but taking nourishment while planning Larkin's demise. I suspect he was thinking of you and taking his first sip of your blood during the mating ceremony."

"He refused my blood," Willow tossed back, rejection coating her words.

"He had to, Willow. When Factions mate, they give the other a part of themselves, Mathias received a sample of your magic. However, he is a vampire, who as you know, consumes blood to sustain life. Had he taken your offering, the ritual would be complete and ruined the plan you have for Larkin. He sacrificed his need for the greater good."

Willow opened her eyes to the sound of footfalls coming down the steps behind her. "We haven't much time, Willow. You need to get out of here."

"But how, Dad? I can't control it."

"Your mother planned for this," Orifiel started, looking passed Willow to the steps. "In her room where you found her books is a wooden box containing her pendant."

Willow reached into her pocket, retrieving the necklace. "I found it, but I—"

"Then you have everything you need. Now hurry, Willow. Get out of here before they find you." Orifiel took a final look at the stairs, the light from the torches growing brighter. Gripping Willow's fingers one last time. "Tomorrow night, if it's safe, I need you to bring Zarina and your mother's pendant back here."

"Why?"

"Just promise me you will if it's safe."

"Okay, I promise."

"Good girl, now go."

Orifiel watched as his daughter clutched the pendant before closing her eyes and disappearing. Shifting his body back to his cot, he leaned to the side, taking in the face of his wife as she lay motionless in the cell across the room. Her skin slick with sweat from the fever which had set in earlier, her eyes sunk in and dark. "Hold on a little longer, my love. Our daughter is going to save you."

CHAPTER FOUR

Willow stood in the center of her room, clutching the pendant so hard it was cutting into the skin of her hand. Dropping her body onto the comforter allowing her eyes to close and arms to flail out to the side. She'd been wrong about Mathias and, as much as she hated to admit it, she owed him an apology. Tucking her mother's pendant back in her pocket, she cleared her mind and pictured the door she'd slammed in his face. Mentally twisting the handle, she opened the door finding a brightly lit room on the other side.

"Mathias?" Willow called stepping into the warm glow of the room, the décor just as spectacular as her parents. "You have every reason not to talk to me ever again, but I came here to apologize."

Willow ghosted her fingers along the back of the wooden chair closest her, the exotic smell of cloves hitting her nose and making her feel at home. Coming to stand in the center of the room, her eyes follow the lines of the room up the cream-colored walls to the crown molding of the cathedral ceilings, coming to rest on the intricate paintings of baby Angels above her.

Warm fingers caressed the skin along her arm, dancing their way from her fingertips to the juncture of her neck and shoulder, sliding her hair to the side. The smell of cloves intensified as a pair of lips brushed the shell of her ear, the hard lines of his body melting into hers. "Your doubt in me is no fault of your own, but of the seed Larkin planted in your gorgeous head. Something I will work hard to remedy if you will allow." The vibration of his voice does such delicious things to her and she prayed it would never change.

Spinning toward him, Willow too his face between her palms, "Please don't say his name, he's stolen enough from us." Crushing her lips against his, freeing herself as she stepped out of her comfort zone and into the realm of pleasure created by her need for the man holding her. Gripping the hair at the back of his neck, she wrapped her fingers in the soft curls she found there. A moan left her throat as Mathias challenged her for control of the kiss, his hands roaming over her back and neck, dipping his right hand into the waist band of her jeans, the feel of her flesh there too great a temptation and he quickly retreated.

Leaning her forehead against his chin, "Tell me it will always be like this." Willow begged, catching the wooden cross dangling from a cord around his neck.

"From what I understand, yes."

Willow pulled back, staring confused into the blue eyes she's grown to love. "Understand?"

Mathias smiled down at her, enjoying her ignorance of the Faction world and his responsibility in sharing the wonderment of each new discovery she had. "*Yes, Beauteous. I've never mated before, but from my observation and the little time I've had with you, yes, I will always crave you.*"

Her fingers migrated to the wood cross, honesty echoing in his words and filling her heart with more love than she could ever imagine. She'd thank her father tomorrow when she saw him, grateful he'd shown her the truth and not allowed her to toss this away.

Tucking her fingers under his cross, an errant thought entered her mind. "*I thought vampires had an aversion to wooden crucifixes?*"

Mathias reached up, taking her fingers in his, "*Afraid not. This was a gift from my father.*"

"*The prior Coven leader?*"

"*No.*" *Shifting them to one of the sofas in the room, relishing the comforts of his home which had been locked away since his exile when Larkin and Ophelia took over. Mathias couldn't wait to bring Willow here for real, carrying her across the threshold after marrying her in front of their friends and family, taking her upstairs to the bed he would prepare for her. Once the Factions were settled, he'd take her around the world, introducing her to the other Covens. But first, he had to open up to her, clarify the visions she saw of his past, to ensure the hiccup they'd survived didn't happen again.*

"*I was born in a small village outside of what is now known as Yorkshire in seventeen fourteen. My brother came less than a year later and our twin sisters three years after, who, regretfully, did not see their first birthday due to a smallpox outbreak which nearly wiped out our village. From the time I could stand, I worked the fields alongside my parents, growing every morsel of food we placed in our mouths. My parents were devoted Catholics, loading us up every Sunday to attend Mass no matter the weather or how much work was left in the fields. When I was about nine, I told my parents I wanted to be a priest when I grew up. They informed our priest of my desire, who took me under his wing and into the church to begin my studies. My absence in helping with the fields took its toll on my father, who collapsed from the heat one day near the end of the harvest. The priest refused to let me go home and help my family, forcing my mother to finish the season alone as Kieran had contracted typhoid and was extremely ill. That winter, we gained a new priest, one who was even crueler than the original. He would beat me if I couldn't recall something or refuse to let me eat or drink until I had all of my work done. When spring came and the blessing of the fields, he refused to allow me to greet my family. As I stood beside him, I heard one of my neighbors behind me whispering how my mother looked good considering the loss of my father. I would later learn from Kieran, my absence impacted my family so severely there wasn't enough food to last the winter. My father chose to starve so that my mother and brother could eat. The priest was nearly finished with the blessing when a cloud of dust floated in bringing with it a group of vampires, out to strengthen their numbers by collecting young men. As you saw in the vision, the priest begged for his life, holding up this crucifix and rebuking Satan. Alaric grabbed the crucifix, severing the priest's head in the process. He spotted me standing to the side, grabbed me by the robes and hoisted me onto the back of his horse. My mother tried to save Kieran, but one of Alaric's men killed her, taking my brother and disappearing into the night. The next day, when the Coven came together, I found Kieran. Alaric allowed us to remain together, calling me his Little Priest due to the clothing I wore. After a while he dropped the Little and changed it to Priestly which Kieran and I adopted as our surname. For years, we worked for him, befriending other boys and luring them back to the camp. Learning from other vampires how to fight and what women were all about. Alaric took me under his wing, showed me what it was to lead a Faction. Just after my twenty-third birthday, the plague broke out, killing thousands of people. Alaric couldn't bear to lose me, so he turned Kieran and myself. We spent the next hundred years traveling around the world, learning new cultures and sampling everything they had to offer. Kieran fell in love with music, quickly mastering every instrument he picked up, forming a band with several of the other vampires in the Coven."*

"After so many years of endless traveling, Kieran and I wanted something more permanent and in a place with no history, bathed in mystery."

"New Orleans," Willow added, her voice soft as she twisted the crucifix around in her fingers.

"Yes, although it was nothing like what you see today."

"What, no Brew Masters?"

Mathias loved her sense of humor, able to pull him from the dark and dreary with a single smile. Flipping her over, laying his hard body over hers. "No, there were a number of settlements, but I don't want to talk about any of that."

"No?"

Shaking his head slowly, maintaining hunger-filled eye contact, Mathias lowered his lips to hers, drinking in the beautiful creature made exclusively for him. He so desperately wanted to push ahead to the eve of her birthday, claiming her in front of Larkin and the rest of his cronies and then ripping his head off and shitting down his throat for touching what's i his. For now, Mathias would settle for having her here in this world created within her dreams. He was free to love her here, show her what their nights together would be like, while keeping within the rules of Faction mating.

Willow craved the way Mathias touched her, lived for the colorful words he would whisper in her ear as his fingers mapped her body. There was no apprehension of being exposed with him, no worry of doing or saying the wrong thing to upset him. Just pleasure upon layers of pleasure as his lips traveled down her neck and between her breasts. His skill caused her back to arch as he wrapped those glorious lips of his around her nipple, using precious amounts of suction to pull a wanton moan from her lips as he pulled her pants and panties down her hips. No embarrassment or need to hide came to her as Mathias sat back on his heels, slipping her jeans down over her knees, tossing them to the floor before spreading her wide, running a single finger along her slit.

Mathias marveled at how ready for him his mate was, her comfort level not something he anticipated, but was grateful for. He'd been between the thighs of countless women, usually to take a meal, but sex was generally on the menu and something he never declined. He recalled with clarity the first time he'd witnessed such an intimate act when Alaric decided it was time to show him how to truly please a woman while taking your fill of her. Running his nose between Willow's folds, taking in the scent of her innocence, lapping his tongue at the sweet taste of her.

Willow could feel the wave building, the pressure inside of her increasing with each brush of his glorious tongue, the heightened passion as he hummed around her tight bundle. She's close, oh so close, as she reached down spearing her fingers into the hair at the side of his head, the blue of his eyes adding so much more to her need for him. With her breathing, rapid, almost panting, she could feel it, the ripple of the wave as it began its crest. Her back arched once again, as her fingers tug with purpose on the silky strands of Mathias's dark hair in her grip. Willow screamed as her legs began to tremble, Mathias increasing his pace.

Her body began to shake, but not as a result of Mathias's tongue, and as the room filled with light and her eyes shot open, she saw a meaty hand on her shoulder gripping her hard enough to leave a mark.

Larkin stood over her, his reptile eyes glowering down at her.

Looking around the room, Willow was relieved to see she was still dressed in the same clothes from last night, minus her jeans, and Mathias is nowhere in sight. "What are you doing in here?"

Larkin stood to his full height, a scowl developing between his scaly brow. "You were screaming, Willow. Are you okay?"

Sitting up, Willow scooted to the head of the bed, leaning against the headboard, still painfully aroused. Mathias swore inside her head, calling Larkin a smelly fucking beast.

"I'm fine, thank you for waking me. By the looks of it, I've overslept."

"Are you sure? Your screams were pretty intense."

Mathias laughed inside her head, *"Of course her screams were intense, you asshat. I was licking her tight pussy."* His deep voice served to increase the wetness between her thighs.

Standing from the bed, Willow caught Larkin's appreciative look at her naked legs. Needing to distract him, *"Forgive me, Mathias. What I'm about to say is a lie."* She warned silently inside her head before reaching into the cotton of her panties, coating her fingers with slick juices Mathias created.

"I was dreaming about you, Larkin." Stepping forward, she took her glistening fingers and slides them between his lips. "Any further questions as to why I was screaming?"

With a quirked eyebrow, Willow stepped by him, unable to turn around as she couldn't allow him to see the disgust on her face. Swaying her hips as she walked into the bathroom, leaning against the closed door, smiling triumphantly when she heard Larkin curse before stomping out of the room and down the steps.

"Willow Morganti, you are a force to be reckoned with. Remind me to remain on your good side."

"Zarina says I'm my mother's daughter for sure."

"Without a doubt. Now, if you will excuse me, I have a pressing matter needing my immediate attention as a result of Larkin's rather rude interruption."

"Want some help with that?"

"Soon, Beauteous, soon."

Willow felt Mathias disconnect as she shrugged off her clothes, stepping hurriedly into the shower. Her mate wasn't the only one with a matter screaming to be handled, and just like the blue-eyed man of her dreams, she'd be handling it herself.

CHAPTER FIVE

Entering the library, Willow found Brynn pacing the floor, a worried look on her face. Stopping abruptly, she studied the haggard face of the Witch, concerned that perhaps she'd overheard what happened upstairs.

"What's wrong?"

Brynn halted her footing, spinning to face Willow, looking in both directions before whispering in the lowest voice possible. "You have a visitor."

"What, who?" Willow questioned, not bothering to lower her voice as Brynn had.

Motioning for her to be quiet, Brynn once again looked in both directions, as if waiting for someone to jump out and catch her. "A man, a handsome one. Called himself Nixx."

"Nixx is here?"

"Yes, he's in the foyer."

"And you left him there?"

Willow tore out of the library as if she were on fire, skirting around Saige who stood in the hall, a tray of tea in her hands. Nixx was the only friend Willow ever had and she couldn't wait to tell him of Mathias, the other Factions and her role in it all.

Running as fast as she could, Willow called out his name before breaking through the foyer, finding Nixx standing in front of the fireplace his head tipped back staring at her mother's painting. Standing beside him, it felt as if a million years had passed since the last time they were together. Memories of the days where they would sneak off together, spending time doing ordinary things young people do, came flooding back. Nixx had been instrumental in introducing her to modern technology and movies she was forbidden from watching under Evanora's strict rules. Brynn was correct, Nixx was a handsome man, with his blonde, curly hair and deep-set eyes. He'd always had a lanky build, even after investing in a home gym, Nixx never formed the muscles they saw on several celebrities.

"She looks a lot like you," Nixx spoke, jolting Willow from the memory of teasing him about his lack in muscle tone after working out daily for several weeks. Having heard the same observation from so many people over the last few days, Willow skipped over the comment and dove into the question burning on her tongue.

"What are you doing here? How did you find me?"

Nixx remained facing the fireplace, turning his head in Willow's direction, his violet eyes gleaming back at her. "Well, when I went over to your house to check on you, I found the house unlocked and the garage door wide open with the convertible missing. I figured you went to the grocery store or to check on your merchandise. When you were still gone the following day, I tried your cellphone, but it went right to voicemail."

Reaching into his pocket, Willow lowered her attention to his hand where her lost cellphone sat in the center of his upturned palm. Her joy was short lived as she took in the broken screen and missing case. The once treasured gift looked as if it had been run over and left for dead.

"I tried tracking it, but as you can see the battery was damaged, rendering it useless."

Lifting the phone from Nixx's hand, "I'm so sorry. One minute I had it out to call a tow truck and the next it was gone." Willow felt horrible for her role in the destruction of something so expensive. Ready with an offer to repay him as she handed it back.

"It's okay, Willow," Nixx shrugged his shoulders. "For whatever reason, the stupid thing came back to life, sending me an alert this morning. When I saw where it was pinging from, I couldn't believe my eyes, so I jumped in my car and drove as fast as I could all the way here."

Willow opened her arms in an invitation for a hug, a

watery smile on her face. "I'm so glad you came, Nixx. I missed you like crazy." Losing herself in the embrace, she closed her eyes tight and focused on the familiar feeling.

"You'll never know how relieved I was than when I pulled up to the garage and saw your aunt's convertible up on the lift."

Separating, "I wanted to call you, but I never memorized your number. The phone in the shop doesn't recognize speed-dial."

"No, I guess it doesn't." Nixx placed a kiss to her forehead, something he'd done before they parted ways for as long as she could recall. The familiar scent of home drifted off him, the damp earth smell of the swamp.

"The good news in all of this is when I spoke with Mr. Merchant," Nixx tipped his head to the back of the room, Willow followed until her eyes landed on Mr. Merchant standing in the corner, his newsy hat gripped in his fingers. "I was able to call my uncle, who owns a salvage yard not three hours from here. They have the hoses you need to get the car back on the road."

Willow dropped her hand from Nixx, turning in Mel's direction. "Mr. Merchant, Brynn didn't mention you were here, what a pleasant surprise." Willow wasn't certain what to make of Mel. While he looked the same as he did the last time she saw him, he was married to Opal and therefore couldn't be trusted. Thinking back, Willow recalled something Zarina mentioned of how fairies were immune from spells and yet greedy as they come. With no noticeable difference in his appearance, and the odd way Brynn had acted, could Mel be Lymrick?

"Please, Willow, call me Mel. Mr. Merchant makes me feel old."

"Of course." She laughed before turning her attention back to Nixx whose face was contorted in confusion.

"Who is Brynn?"

Grabbing Nixx by the arm, she invited him to take a seat as she told him of coming to New Orleans and finding her mother's house. Willow purposely left out the part where she'd discovered how real Vampires and Witches were and how all of those creatures in the movies he'd watched with her were living around them. She told him of why she resembled the woman in the painting so much and how Saige had inadvertently saved her from living inside a coffee shop. "Back to what you mentioned earlier, this uncle of yours and parts for my car."

Nixx stood from the couch, pulling Willow with him, causing her to giggle from the same antics they shared as young children. "Yeah, my uncle had everything Mel needed and I was going to see if you wanted to come along,"

Willow knew Larkin would never let her out the front door, however her concern wasn't with her safety, but Nixx's. She assumed with a flick of her wrist and a few carefully chosen words, if Larkin tried anything, she could have him withering on the floor in the blink of an eye. But how would she explain it to Nixx? Furthermore, there was the much bigger issue of saving the Factions, especially Mathias and her parents.

"I would love nothing more than a road trip; however I gave my word I would help out in the store to earn money to pay Mr. Merchant." Shaking her head, "I mean, Mel. I'll need to check with Saige to see if I've earned enough money to cover his fee and the cost of the parts from your uncle."

Mel stepped further into the room, tossing his hat on the coffee table beside Nixx. "I'm sure you have. From what I hear, business is good, and with the ball in a few days."

Willow struggled to recall even one customer outside of Lincoln and Daragis who came into the store but came up empty.

"Wait, a ball?" Nixx laughed, stealing Willow's attention back to the conversation. "Isn't your birthday in a couple of days?"

"Yes, but I'm sure it won't take long for Mel to put the parts into my car and I can head back—"

"Are you kidding me, Willow? We're in New Orleans and you'll be of legal drinking age." Nixx grabbed her hands, pulling her to his chest before spinning her around. "We aren't going home, Willow. We're going to celebrate."

Nixx hugged her again before heading out the front door with Mr. Merchant, a promise to get the parts and return tomorrow. Willow offered to let him stay at the house, but

Nixx declined, admitting he'd gotten a room at a hotel not far and would spend his first evening in the French Quarter checking out the local flavors. Sealing his words with a wink, he left Willow with a new impression of her old friend.

BRYNN AND SAIGE WERE UNUSUALLY QUIET AS THEY ground Wormwood and Ripplewood for the spell. Willow purposely made no mention of the guest from earlier, allowing the expanding fear of what's to come. Instead, she kept her smile to herself, picturing in her mind instead of how the pair would act when the hour of judgement arrived.

Larkin stayed away the remainder of the day, Willow assumed it had to do with her sexual innuendo from this morning, or perhaps he too, was concerned with Mr. Merchant's visit. When the calm evening light filtered through the windows, Saige and Brynn slipped out of the library and into their perspective bedrooms, neither of them bothering to offer her the standard cup of pre-bedtime tea.

Just before midnight, as Willow made her way upstairs, she paused on the landing taking a look at the rooms where the pair slept, finding doors closed and not an ounce of light filtering from beneath. She smiled to herself as she continued on, finding the door to her mother's room visible tonight.

Stepping inside, she hurried across the room, dropping to her knees to retrieve the book she needed from under the bed. Flipping through the pages, she located the spell she needed, stood to her full height and began chanting the words silently in her head. Her birthmark and fingers tingled as she visualized the words on the page. Opening her eyes, Willow was beyond proud when she found Zarina standing at the foot of her mother's bed with a confused look on her face.

"What's wrong?" Zarina questioned, her eyes never leaving Willow's.

"I hate waiting until midnight to do this." Willow reasoned, thinking of all the useless tasks she performed today while waiting for the house to fall asleep.

"For now, it's necessary. Now, tell me what's wrong, I know you didn't bring me here for the famous tea."

"I found my parents. My dad said to find you and bring to him."

Zarina rounded the end of the bed, taking Willow's hand in hers. "Then what are we waiting for? Take me to them."

Reaching in her pocket, Willow retrieved her mother's pendant, slipping it around her neck. The tingling in her fingers intensified and the birthmark shifted to the cool sensation she felt when she became angry and stopped time. Gripping Zarina's fingers, "Hold on tight, this is my first time doing this with a passenger."

AVENGING ANGEL

The tingling in her fingers morphed into a hum as the room shifted from luxurious comforts to a dark and dingy room. Zarina immediately let go of her hand, calling out her mother's name before running across the room and dropping to her knees beside a woman lying still on a makeshift bed.

Willow's heart falls in her chest as she takes in the ghostly appearance, the frail, bone-thin body of the woman from the painting. Her eyes were closed, sunken in, with deep purple rings around them. Guilt blanketed her from lack of seeking out her mother yesterday, spending all of her time with her father instead of inquiring about her clearly ill mother.

"Zarina will fix her, just as you did me." Pushing away the single tear escaping from her lids, Willow could feel her father approach from behind, the gentleness of his hand on her shoulder as he pulled her flush to his chest. She bathed in his comfort as she watched Zarina let her hands hover over her mother's body, chanting words too low for Willow to hear.

"Your mother had a visitor the week before you were born. Pallen, the Coven leader from a neighboring state, had a premonition of how Ophelia and her sisters planned to steal your mother's magic. I offered to put an end to her, but your mother refused, feeling the vision the Warlock had could be false or invented. I begged her to let me do something, but she wrapped her arms around my neck and kissed me like she always did, assuring me she had a backup plan."

CAYCE POPONEA

"Wait, why would Opal want my mother's dark magic? Isn't it the opposite of her Earth Magic?"

From across the room, Zarina stood to her feet, eyes squinting as she twisted her head in question. "Earth Magic? Opal was never an Earth Witch. She and her sisters come from a longline of Black Magic Witches. Your mother punished her by taking away her magic after she committed a forbidden act."

Willow's curiosity was off the charts, feeling lost as every turn seemed to reveal more truth of the people around her. "Which was?"

"Seducing and then subsequently killing a Dragon, draining his blood and using it for sorcery by giving life to a cursed creature."

Zarina held up her hand as Willow opened her mouth to confirm what she already knew. "That's a story for your father to tell. I need your mother's pendant; she's been separated from her magic for too long and I need to return it to her."

The question on Willow's lips was forgotten as she moves to join her mother. "Not now, Willow." Zarina stopped her.

"But I need to see her."

Zarina reached around Willow's neck, unclasping the pendant and stepping back. "Tomorrow my child. She'll be stronger then and able to greet your properly. Besides, your father has something he needs to show you."

Nodding in surrender, Willow watched as Zarina returned to her mother's side, carefully fastening the pendant around her neck, hovering her hands over head and silently chanting.

"Come on, Willow." Her father offered, holding his hand out for hers. "It's time you have a look at the truth for yourself."

CHAPTER SIX

Willow found herself in the center of the French Quarter outside the house she'd recently come to call home. Looking up at the fading paint and crumbling brick, the structure looked nothing like the first time she saw it. Her father stood to the right of her, his eyes full of pain and regret as he took in the dilapidated home he'd shared with his wife.

Lights from an approaching car reflected off the metal supports of the house, gaining the pairs attention. Willow watched as the door opens revealing a much more naïve girl who stared in wonderment at the house, granted those eyes were glamoured with Opal's special tea. Still holding her father's hand, she waited as the lights in the shop go out and the house became still, recalling the anxiety of her first night behind those walls.

"Willow, look." Orifiel motioned to the four figures standing in the shadows at the edge of the house.

"Do you think it's her?" Brynn spoke, while staring up at the window on the second floor, the same one Willow caught a glimpse of herself staring hopelessly out of before the curtain fluttered shut.

"She has the mark, and the power spilling from her is like no other witch in the city." Opal added, her focus like the others on the now dark window above.

"Even…" Saige started, but Opal held up a hand to stop her.

"Yes, even her. I've been able to channel a small sample, which gave the spell on the house a boost." Saige said, turning from the window and toward the other three.

"Let's hope it holds, because if she sees…"

Opal shook her head as she too turned from the house. *"Do not question me, sister. I've channeled more magic than you will see in a thousand lifetimes."*

Saige lowered her head, staring intently at the tip of her shoes. *"I know. Still, if you think it's really her, then we need to notify his Eminence."*

"Leave him to me, sister. No need to ruffle his feathers if she isn't the one." Brynn stood tall, jealousy coating each of her words leaving Willow without a single doubt who she's referencing. How had she missed the attraction between them?

"Opal has waited a long time for you to come back to the city," Willow's father began, tipping his head in the direction of the four still standing near the alley. "She, alongside Saige, have planned for the day they could take their revenge against your mother."

"What about Brynn, where does she fit in all of this?" Willow couldn't believe she'd been fooled by the blue-haired Witch twice. First with Larkin, now with her sibling association to the other two.

"Brynn has been in infatuated with Larkin since she first laid eyes on him." Orifiel huffed, leaving Willow the impression there was something wrong with the union. "Come on, sweetheart, this is something you have to see for yourself."

Willow nodded absently as she stared at the fourth figure. Viktor, her least favorite of all Larkin's men, stood hands on hip as the three other departed ways, keeping his focus on the backside of the Witch closest him. Taking her father's hand once again, Willow couldn't shake the feeling something was very wrong with this picture.

The music of the French Quarter faded away, replaced by the agonizing scream of a woman in severe pain. Willow turned her attention to a makeshift shelter under a fallen tree where two women hunkered down, one lying on her back with her knees in the air, while the other stood between them, encouraging her to push. Willow watched as the woman on her back cried out again as she bore down, her face so red it was nearly purple, a baby's cry following shortly after.

"Tell me it's okay." The woman begged, reaching for the tiny baby she'd just given birth to.

The second woman swaddled the tiny baby in what appeared to be rags, swaying back and forth in an effort to soothe the tiny cries. *"He's just fine. Looks like his beautiful mum, not an ounce of his father in him."*

Orifiel leaned down to his daughter's ear, trying his best not to startle the poor girl. "Larkin's birth was not a joyous event. His mother had traded her body for passage into a place she had no right venturing into. The subsequent pregnancy something she hid from everyone."

"Why? Was his father married or something?" Willow questioned, taking in the baby fidgeting in his mother's arms.

"No, he wasn't married." Orifiel shook his head, "Although it would have been easier for his mother if he had been."

Not waiting for his daughter to inquire, Orifiel shifted time once again, placing them in the center of a thick forest. "Look to your left, Willow. What do you see?"

Following her father's outstretched hand, she noticed two figures leaning against a massive bolder. Both are naked from the waist down, the taller of the two bent over the smaller one and its clear by the thrusting of hips they are engaged in heated sex.

Willow points at the couple, "Is that...?" Trailing off, unable to believe her eyes.

"It is."

"Wow."

"Wow indeed, sweetheart." Orifiel laughed. "Wow indeed."

Willow leaned into her father as the couple reached their climax, holding back the laughter begging to be set free. She would save the memory, keeping it hidden until the time was right.

"I have one more to show you before we need to get you back upstairs." Orifiel sorrowfully admitted, wanting nothing more than to spend more time bonding with his grown daughter. How beautiful she'd become, the spitting image of her mother, blessed with the same poise and grace, and hopefully incredible power.

Willow held tight to her father's hand. Now that she'd learned of his existence, she shuddered at the thought of letting him go, focusing instead on the rolling hills around her.

"Where are we?" The question barely left Willow's lips before the sound of a released arrow buzzed by her, landing with a thud in the center of a target not ten feet from them. Turning in the direction from where the arrow came, Willow found two men dressed in Medieval clothing, a bow in each of their hands. Astonishment colored her face as her eyes took in Larkin's human appearance. Pink cheeks of youth split in half with a triumphant smile, his hair much longer than his current length, but Willow assumed it was customary for the time. Larkin was nowhere near as muscular as he is today, however, Willow understood the reason behind it.

"Early seventeen hundred, give or take a year." A second arrow wizzed by them followed by the deep laughter of the two men.

"I win again, Brother." Larkin shouted, crossing the distance to the target, pulling his arrow from the center of the first arrow, having split it in half to the hilt.

"I let you win, Larkin." Viktor argued, shoulder checking Larkin as the two sat on the hill, pulling what looked to be an apple from a pocket. *"Just as I let you have that wench last night."*

Willow rolled her eyes at their banter, surmising no matter the time period, all men were the same. She tried not the think of all the women in Mathias's past, how many times he and Kieran partook in conversations such as the one in front of her.

"Look in the tree line, Willow. Tell me what you see?"

Searching the area her father pointed to, coming up empty for several passes until a flash of something white caught her gaze. "Is that, Brynn?"

"The one and only," Orifiel tossed, condescension wrapped around each letter.

Like passing a horrific traffic accident, Willow was unable to pull her eyes away from the young woman partially hidden behind the thick vegetation. Her hair so white it glowed in the sun, braided to the side and flowing down her shoulder, around her exposed breast. Brynn too looked different from the woman Willow saw every day, but it was the way her hand was buried between her thighs that imprisoned Willow's attention, not the youthful attributes.

"As I said earlier, Brynn has been infatuated with Larkin from the moment she laid eyes on him. When his mother brought him to this castle, Brynn found work as a healer to the King so she could remain close."

Scoffing, "Ironically, it was her infatuation which opened my eyes to the pair of them, subsequently meeting Zarina and ultimately Mathias."

"I know. After you left, I took a look for myself and found Larkin doing the same thing outside your window as Brynn is in the weeds."

"Larkin was masturbating outside my window?" Shock riddled Willow for the briefest of time before the need to scrub her skin kicked in, sending a shudder down her body.

"On more than one occasion," Orifiel admitted, the same anger surfacing as when he'd witnessed it the first time. Larkin's days were measured in his opinion, more than ready to see what actions Mathias took against him, once he became aware. Given the added ability their mating connection brought, he felt sorry for his friend, but not enough to take Larkin's side. "That's not the worst of it," Orifiel waved his hand in the air, sliding time forward a few hours. "Brynn may have won Larkin's affections, but it wasn't enough, at least not for her."

Orifiel turned to his daughter, holding back his joviality when her eyes bulged at the couple spread out on the bed. "They share her?"

"Not exactly, Willow. Brynn did indeed capture Larkin's eye and take him to her bed, but she took many men to her bed, including Viktor. Brynn wasn't a stupid woman. She knew at the time the chances of Larkin getting killed in battle were high. So, she sought protection from many men, always keeping them in the dark from one another."

"Protection or not," Willow argued, turning from the scene of Viktor claiming Brynn from behind. "From the look on Viktor's face the first night I arrived in New Orleans, his feelings for Brynn are as deep as the cavern they've imprisoned you in."

WILLOW SAT IN A MASSIVE TUB, A MOUNTAIN OF BUBBLES surrounding her, the feel of Mathias's bare chest against her back.

"I never pictured you as a bubble bath lover kind of guy." She teased, wiggling her body against his hard appendage at the base of her spine.

"I'm a lover of anything that makes the love of my life happy," Mathias professed truthfully, kissing the skin of her shoulder. Willow allowed her head to fall back into the curve of his neck, losing herself in the feelings his touch created in her.

"I can still smell Larkin's stench on you." Mathias swore as he kneaded her right breast.

"I'm sorry, Mathias. I had to do something, and it was the first thing to pop into my head." Taking his hand from her breast, she covered his fingers with hers, locking eyes with him over her shoulder as she spread her lower lips wide and pushed his digits inside her. Placing her lips to his, she guided his fingers over her swollen lips and clit, using his fingers to work herself into a frenzy, climaxing hard when his thumb brushed against her sensitive core, crying out his name as her body jerked from the intensity.

Bringing his hand up and out of the water, pressing both of their fingers past his lips and against his tongue. "Larkin may have tasted me first, but it was you who got to see the end result, something he will never experience."

Mathias pulled his hand free, gripped her wrist and sucked hard on her fingers, licking every drop of her sweet essence.

"You have no idea how badly I want to push into you, feel you quiver around me and scream my name again."

"Then what are you waiting for?"

Mathias spun her around until she's straddling his hips, her core lined up against his aching cock. Palming her face, his blue eyes searching hers. "I've waited hundreds of years, searched though countless women to find my perfect match. I will not do anything to jeopardize having you forever, even if it means denying myself what I want most. Besides, when I do wrap you around me, I want it to be in my bed, and not in my mind."

Knowing Mathias was right, Willow moved to the opposite side of the tub, using the bubbles to camouflage their naked bodies.

"I saw my mother earlier. Well, a glimpse of her anyway."

Mathias reached out, taking Willow's foot in hand, massaging the arch with his thumbs, grateful for her understanding and willingness not to push the envelope. Keeping his eyes trained on her beautiful face as the bubbles provide little resistance to his vampire sight.

"What do you mean a glimpse?"

Willow told him of how ill her mother was and how she left Zarina in the cavern, her father having regained most of his strength now that the ropes were soaked in rose water, not Wolfsbane.

"I nearly forgot to tell you about my friend Nixx coming into town."

"Nixx?" Mathias questioned, moving his fingers to the ball of her foot. "When was this? Is Nixx a guy or girl?"

Willow smiled sweetly at the clearly jealous Mathias, before reaching for his hands to pull herself back to his side of the tub.

"Nixx is my best friend from Florida. He is a guy, but you have nothing to worry about as he doesn't feel for me like you do."

Mathias gripped her waist shifting her to his left side and away from his rock-hard erection. His jealousy was a side effect of the mating, ready to wake from this dream and kill this Nixx with his bare hands.

"He's a guy, Willow. We may come in different packages, but we all want the same thing. He may have hidden it well, but trust me, he's thought about touching you here." His middle finger was buried deep

inside her before he could stop himself, the coordinating thumb rubbing her clit at blurring speed, sending Willow into an instant orgasm.

A CLAP OF THUNDER WOKE WILLOW FROM THE WONDERFUL dream she shared with Mathias, her body still humming from the ministrations of his talented fingers and thumb. Glancing at the clock on her bed-side table, she was surprised to see it was just after three in the morning. Turning back to her view of the ceiling, she snuggled under her covers as the rain fell gently outside, Mother Nature's sweet lullaby encouraging her back to sleep. As Willow closed her eyes, an errant thought entered her mind, forcing her to spring from her bed and cross the room to her balcony.

Pulling back the curtain, Willow silently celebrated when she saw Larkin's post once again empty. How many times had he forbade her to leave this house without him, yet refused to accompany her when she'd requested? Dashing across the room, she shoved her legs and feet in her discarded jeans and shoes before closing her eyes and recalling the words written in the spellbook under her mother's bed.

"Willow, no!" Mathias shouted inside her head. *"Please, Beauteous, for me. Don't do what you're thinking."*

"I'm sorry, Mathias, but I have to."

CHAPTER SEVEN

Lightning flashed through the stained-glass windows, dazzling Willow momentarily with a glimpse of the architecture surrounding her. She'd suspected Larkin's unwillingness to bring her here had more to do with something he was hiding, rather than his claim of protecting her.

"Illuminate," Willow chanted. The candles around the foyer sprung to life, giving her the first real look at the inside of the church she'd longed to visit. She wasn't surprised to see the floor littered with leaves and dirt, or massive chains wrapped around the handles of the doors, keeping prying eyes and inquisitive parishioners outside.

The sound of Willow's footfalls echoed in the church as she made her way to the sanctuary. The dust and debris continued, prohibiting her from seeing the beauty of the room she had no doubt was hidden underneath. As she approached the altar, Willow chanted once again, bringing the few candles still intact to life and a gasp to her throat.

The stone altar sat broken in three pieces as if the hand of God slammed down on the center of it. Thousands of tiny rocks spread out across the raised area like confetti following a shout of surprise. Tears stung her eyes while a battle between hate and anguish raged inside her chest as she stared hard at her father's wings draped over what was left of the crucifix. The damaged wood lay intertwined with the stone from the altar, another victim of the apparent war which occurred here.

Willow blindly reached out, running a shaking finger over the soft feathers of her father's wings, her tears blurring them into a jagged cloud of white. Her birthmark hummed, fingertips glowing a brilliant blue which lit the area around her with such brilliance it was nearly blinding. Angry sobs riddled her body, fueling the growing anger inside of her.

A heavy thud sounded off in the distance, ending Willow's tears but allowing the rage to remain. She listened closely to see if someone was coming or if the storm was growing closer outside.

"Two more days."

Willow dropped her hand, turning her body and taking a determined step in the direction of Larkin's voice. The plan to take him down clouded by her need to make him pay for what he did to her family.

"Two more and then I won't have to smell the stench of her or pretend to fall deeper in love with her. All I want to do is steal the life from her and take what is rightfully mine."

Her steps quickened as she leapt from the raised platform, pulverizing the rocks under the weight of her rage. She had no idea where Larkin was, but every intention of finding him and tossing every ounce of her Angel power against him, reducing him to nothing. She'd never felt this kind of anger before, never had anything worth getting remotely upset about other than her lack of life experience outside of her home. All that had changed. Now she had a lifetime of unread chapters waiting to be written, with one arrogant Gargoyle standing in her way.

Quickening her steps, the burn of her birthmark guiding her way, leading her toward the evil who was about to be returned to Hell where he belonged. As she approached the end of the pews, the thud of heavy footfalls grew closer, her rage narrowing her vision, casting shadows on everything around her. Words to the spell vibrant in her head, however she would say them out loud, taking joy in watching his shocked face as he heard them, then dance over his dead body once her revenge was complete.

Halting her movements, she shifted into a defensive stance, but as she raised her glowing hands, something hit her hard from the left, sending her flying toward the floor, landing in the space between the filthy pews.

"Off lumine," echoed in Willow's ear a second before the candles snap off leaving the room bathed in darkness. A firm hand covered her mouth, a familiar spicy scent reaching her nose as a heavy body covered hers, trapping her to the floor.

"I'm sorry, Willow, but I couldn't let you do this. I know

you want to kill Larkin, so do I, but your parents will perish too if you reveal yourself now." A deep voice hissed in her ear, thick tendrils of the man's hair falling into her face. "Dissipati peribunt."

Willow struggled against the hold of the man as Larkin's boot-clad feet passed mere inches from her. Stilling her movements, she watched as he and several of his men carried blue stained bags in their hands, old ropes dangling from the drawstring openings.

When Larkin reached where Willow once stood, he tipped his head back, clearing his throat before spitting on the wings. "I'm going to fuck her raw, Old Man. Make you watch as I split the bitch in half."

The man holding Willow down waited until well after Larkin and his men left the room before removing the spell. "Okay, Willow, I'm going to remove my hand, but I need you to swear you won't scream and bring that sadistic bastard back here."

Willow thought about agreeing and then doing what he forbade her just to get Larkin back so she could destroy him. But as the thought developed in her mind, something deep inside rippled, telling her to follow the man's instructions. Nodding her head, the man slowly pulled his hand away, lifting himself from her, and then helping her up.

Spinning around words full of venom fresh on her tongue quickly drifted away as she took in the face of the man who'd stopped her. "I know you…" Willow trailed off, unsure of where she'd seen his face before.

Smiling, "We've never officially met." Holding out his hand to her, "My name is Thaddeus Grinwald. I'm friends with your father."

The photo from a shelf in Zarina's cavern popped into her mind, the man beside her father now standing before her.

"Thaddeus? The Coven leader?"

"Not officially, no, but I'll let your mother explain that to you. Listen, I know you have a million questions and I'd love to answer them all, but we need to get out of here before Larkin discovers you're not in your bed."

"How did you know I was here?" Willow ignored his ominous statement, unwilling to leave this spot based on what the man said. Considering the magic he'd shown he was definitely someone with pull or working for Larkin.

"That one I can answer," holding out his hand palm up. "See for yourself, Willow."

Squaring her shoulders, she looked from the man's hand back to his face, her eyebrow raised high in challenge.

"You can't seriously think I've been your father's friend all this time and not taken a trip in time with him."

"I can think anything I choose. Besides, I have no proof you are indeed my father's friend and not another one of Larkin's supporters."

"Yes, you do," Thaddeus challenged. "Had you suspected

I was one of Larkin's, you would have chosen your words more carefully. Now come on, we're wasting time."

Willow would never admit to her blunder, or confess she knew him from the photo in Zarina's cavern. With a faux roll of her eyes, Willow placed her hand in his. The room around them disappearing the second their skin touched, transforming into the familiar décor of Brew Masters. Her father and the man holding her hand sat in a booth at the back of the bar.

"Orifiel came to me after your mother met with Pallen, the Coven leader from Alabama. He and I agreed to put measures in place to protect the queen."

The scene shifted again, this time to an alley behind her house, the windows from the library full of light illuminating the three figures standing in the yard.

"You're sure you felt someone performing magic?"

"Positive, and by the feel of it, the power is fresh and raw."

"Keep the shield up, I have a plan to bring out whomever dares to do magic in this town without my permission."

"So you betrayed him?" Willow seethed, the tingle in her fingers springing to life.

"Hold on," Thaddeus cautioned, gripping her hand tighter, the energy flowing off her so painful he struggled to keep hold. "Just watch."

Willow's body shook from the adrenaline pulsing through her body, sweat dripping down her back and forehead, her fingers poised to split this traitor in half. She watched as the third figure looked to the side, catching Saige as she perused Thaddeus's body as if trying to memorize it.

"Are you and Saige…" Willow drifted off, unable to wrap her mind around someone as handsome as Thaddeus wanting to be with someone as vile as Saige. Her mind drifted back to the dinner party with the faux Faction leader and the way Saige reacted to Thaddeus's name. Was she smitten?

"Mated?" He scoffed, "Hardly, not that she would oppose it." Tipping his head back to the scene as he moved to leave while the other two remain. Opal wrapped a comforting arm around Saige, pulling her into a warm embrace. "*Soon my, dear sister. With Evanora gone, his Eminence will be yours soon.*"

Willow's heart fell at the mention of her guardian; however, her curiosity is piqued at the name Opal called Thaddeus. "Eminence?"

"Yes, a huge honor I suppose," shrugging his shoulders. "If it wasn't a complete lie." Gripping her fingers once again, the back alley and Saige's long face disappeared, the living room of her mother's home forming around them. Her father sat on the sofa, her mother round with pregnancy beside him, their hands clasped tight. Thaddeus and a much younger looking Evanora sitting beside him, their close proximity resembling her parents.

"*I wish there was another way.*"

"Cerise, we've looked at it from every angle. The only other solution is..."

"I know, I know, but I can't have Ophelia killed based on a vision, no matter how much I want to." Cerise rubbed her swollen belly as Orifiel kissed the top of her head.

"I will take care of her, I swear on my life," Evanora rose from her seat, Thaddeus holding on to her hand until the last possible second. *"And when the time is right, I'll send the signal."*

Cerise's eyes filled with tears as she reached out for Evanora. *"This is asking too much; I can't separate the two of you."*

"You did not ask, Cerise. I love you and this little girl growing inside you. This city needs the both of you to survive in order to thrive and make it a place worth living for all of the Factions. Besides, Cerise, you are sacrificing the most of all of us. Something only a true leader would do."

Willow's eyes remained fixed on the couples, "She knew they would take me, that she would miss out on everything."

"Yes."

"And my father, he knew they would take his wings?"

Thaddeus swallow hard, "No, not his wings. Larkin surprised us both with that one."

Willow fell silent as she looked at the group, the loving, yet worried face of Evanora in particular. "All this time, she wasn't keeping me from living life, she was keeping me alive."

"Yes, but that wasn't all."

"What do you mean?"

"Come on, I have one last thing to show you. Prepare yourself, what you're about to see is unsettling."

CHAPTER EIGHT

A COOL BREEZE BLEW PIECES OF HAIR OVER WILLOW'S face, the goosebumps created by the chill in the air not enough to bring her out of the trance she'd been in since bidding Thaddeus goodbye. He'd been right, as the scene she'd watched play out opened her eyes and left a gaping hole in her heart she wasn't certain would ever heal. Mathias gave her his condolences as he too watched the scene unfold, swearing he will do anything he could to avenge her the moment he was free from his black hole prison. She was holding on to the assurance Thaddeus gave her, telling her to delay the spell until she heard from him again, a signal she wouldn't be able to ignore.

"Willow? Baby, are you okay?" Larkin's attempt at gentleness was more like sandpaper on an open wound than the faux concern cluttering his voice. "I've been calling your name for twenty minutes."

Pulling herself back to the present, "I'm fine, really." She tried to smile, pushing past the images forever burned in her mind. "Just mentally preparing for tonight."

Willow tried not to flinch when Larkin placed his talons on her shoulder, followed by his half-hearted attempt at a massage. "You're so tense, sweetheart," he whispered in her ear, the edge of his scaled cheek brushing against hers. "I'd love to work these kinks out, but your friend Nixx is downstairs waiting on you."

Jumping to her feet, Willow spun around searching Larkin's face for any trace of deception, "Nixx is here? What about Mel and my car?"

Perplexed, Larkin shook his head. "No, just your gentleman friend. Willow, are you alright?"

Not bothering to offer an answer, Willow pushed passed him, running through her bedroom and down the stairs, skidding to a stop outside the kitchen when she heard Nixx's signature laugh. Cautiously entering the room, she found her friend sitting beside a girl she'd never met, as Saige set plates of food on the bar in front of the pair, her face wide in smile as she glanced in Willow's direction.

"Good morning, Willow. You look as if you slept well."

Nixx turned in her direction, placing a kiss to the head of the giggling girl beside him before standing to greet her.

"She always looks this good, no sleep or makeup required." Nixx crossed the room, placing an unceremonious kiss to her cheek. Willow quirked an eyebrow at him as this wasn't their standard greeting.

"Good morning to you too, Nixx. Are you going to introduce me to your friend?"

Nixx held her gaze for several seconds, cocking his head to the side and sending her a wink. In all the time he'd known Willow, she'd never shown any interest in him romantically, yet the first time he brought another girl into the picture, the claws appeared.

"When I got back to town early this morning, I was too wired up to go to bed. The streets called to me, begging I join the party as it had just begun. I came by, but all the lights were out, so I went down the street, where I found this exquisite creature dancing on a table."

Willow was all too familiar with how loud the streets of New Orleans could be when they called your name, having ignored them for as long as she could before stepping onto the path which gave her Mathias.

"The moment Jade and I locked eyes, I knew I had to introduce myself."

"And here you are," Willow finished for him, crossing the small space and extending a hand to the golden skinned girl devouring the food on her plate. "I'm Willow, Nixx's friend from Florida. Pleasure to meet you."

Jade glanced from Willow's fingertips to her face and back again, the scowl on her face telling Willow she viewed her as a threat, a measure which couldn't be further from the truth. Barely touching her hand, the half-naked girl returned to her breakfast, a snide "hey," leaving her lips before shoving a fork full of eggs into her mouth.

Spinning on Nixx, "Did Mr. Merchant give you any idea how long before my car would be running again?"

Nixx stepped around Willow, flipping his chair and straddling it. "Tomorrow at the earliest. The hoses my uncle had weren't quite the right size, but Mel said he could make it work."

Tomorrow, Willow thought, her reasons for leaving having changed dramatically. She still wanted to enjoy the city, yet the quietness of her home in Florida was calling her once again.

"Beauteous, I will show you the real New Orleans. Let you drink whatever you want, eat whatever strikes your fancy, and be by your side for anything you need."

A warmth rushed over her at the implications of Mathias's honesty. The reality of her lack of plans beyond the eve of her birthday crashing into her.

"Listen, Willow, Jade is throwing a party with her roommates tonight. Why don't I pick you up around six? We can grab something to eat and hit a few bars before going over there so the two of you can get to know each other better."

Willow didn't have to look in Jade's direction to see the expression on her face, she could feel the daggers the jealous girl was shooting her way.

"As great as that sounds, Nixx. Willow has plans this evening," Larkin deadpanned. With all the distractions in the room, Willow had failed to hear him enter the room.

"Wow, Willow," Nixx stood from the chair, crossing his arms and puffing out his chest. "Traded one warden for another, did we?"

Larkin towered over Nixx, his appearance demonic against the sun-kissed skin and blonde hair of Nixx. Mathias huffed inside Willow's head, sending a mental picture of him sitting in a chair with his feet planted on a table, his arms crossed as if enjoying a sporting event on, increasing the warm sensation filling her.

"Take your conflicts outside, Gentlemen. I won't have your battle destroying my home." Saige spoke from her spot at the sink, her face full of unwavering authority.

"My house," Willow spoke before she could stop herself, gaining the attention of the entire room. The look on Saige's face softened, her hand reaching for the steeping cup of tea to her right.

"Sorry, my choice of words were out of habit and not meant to offend."

Ignoring the slip-of-the-tongue as Saige claimed, turning to Nixx instead. "Larkin is correct, I do have plans for this evening." The excuse barely left her lips before a conceited huff made its way out of Larkin's chest, ruffling Nixx's coif.

"However, I would love to have you escort me to my party

tomorrow night." Flashing her eyes to Jade, ready to warn her the party would be in Willow's honor and not somewhere she might find fun, only to find her enamored with her phone, her thumbs a blur at the speed of her typing.

"But Willow," Larkin gripped her arm with his talon, his hold tight enough to have Mathias swearing profanities inside her head. "I was planning to escort you. After all—"

"Nixx is my dearest friend, Larkin." Willow interrupted. "Besides, it would appear prearranged if I come dangling from your arm, and then announced my choice."

"Willow is correct," Saige added, sliding into a chair beside Nixx. "The other Factions would scream favoritism, demanding a formal hearing before The Council. Plus, this would give Willow time with her friend, introducing him to the life she has here in the Quarter."

Larkin nodded before dropping his hand, turning on his haunches and leaving the room. Had this conversation taken place a few days ago, she would have run after him and tried to reason her decision. That time had passed.

Nixx nudged a still typing Jade on the shoulder but failed to gain her attention. Shrugging, he turned back to face Willow. "New life, huh?"

Willow stood deeper in the crossroads, needing to decide which path to take. "My mother was sort of notorious here in the Quarter, she possessed certain items which could fall to me on my birthday." Needing to remain vague, Willow chose her words carefully, purposely avoiding the word magic.

"Like this house?"

"Among other things," Willow offered. "Listen, Nixx, enjoy your night with Jade. Tomorrow be here at ten, dressed in whatever you have with you and help me ring in my twenty-first birthday."

With a nod of his head and an inquisitive look on his face, Nixx agreed, taking Jade by the arm and ushering her down the hall and out of the house. Willow stood looking down the hall for several minutes after he left, her mind and heart waging war with one another. How in the world was she going to tell him the truth and not send him screaming down the street?

"It isn't hard to see how much you care for him," Saige spoke from behind her. "But he deserves to hear the truth, even if it means you lose him."

CHAPTER NINE

Willow stood facing the painting of her mother, studying the pendant secured around her neck. She'd worked late into the afternoon making sure there was enough Wormwood for the spell to free Larkin. While the work was unnecessary, it gave her something to do, distracting her mind from the impending question of where to go once her parents were freed and the Factions were reunited with their families and businesses.

"Willow, you're supposed to be resting."

Not bothering to look in Larkin's direction, Willow kept her eyes fixed on the pendant as if it would somehow show her the long-term results of whatever choice she made.

"Willow, did you…" Larkin's question drifted off as the room around her began to shake, the sound of shattering glass accompanied the moan of wood, protesting the abrupt movement. Heavy hands grabbed her, tossing her like a rag doll until the world around her shifted into a blur of color and sound. Her breath was ripped from her as her backside collided with something hard. Looking around, Willow regained her breath as she took in the broken glass around her, splinters of wood and an occasional stone.

"Where are we?" Willow demanded, knowing the answer but not wanting a pacing Larkin to know of her prior visit.

"Somewhere safe," he seethed, his footsteps crushing the stone and glass under him to dust. Willow glanced around the room, her eyes landing on the broken window behind Larkin, the crucifix which once hung there now broken in half on the floor, her father's wings buried underneath the splintered wood. Pain gripped her chest as she took in the white feathers lying on the dirty floor without care. The thought of how she shouldn't have listened to Thaddeus entered her mind a second before the bottom of the wings glitter as if possessed by magic. The corner of her mouth curled up, those wings were as fake as the affliction Larkin claimed to suffer from.

"What is going on, Larkin? Why did you bring me here?"

Larkin abruptly stopped, turning his reptile eyes to her. "We were under attack again, one of the Factions was trying to steal you."

"Who?"

Resuming his pacing, "I don't know."

Willow's eyes shifted to the blue-eyed raven sitting on the

edge of the broken window, something white tied to his leg. Turning around, she watched as he flew across the street, landing with ease on the balcony outside her room.

"Larkin, if my house was under attack, then how did you bring me across the street to the church? How did you get passed them?"

Larkin stopped his pacing, turning on Willow and storming to mere centimeters from her face. "Don't tell me you didn't feel the house vibrating?" His breath engulfed her, making her stomach turn from the stench of it. It didn't escape her how he ignored her question, instead shoving his massive size at her in an effort to intimidate her.

"No," Willow lied, praying her voice didn't betray her. "One minute I'm looking at my mother's painting and the next you toss me over your shoulder."

Willow suspected the earthquake like disturbance was the signal Thaddeus spoke of. With her father's wings now gone, she was certain things had progressed with her mother.

"Now take me back home, I need to rest until it's time to perform your spell."

———

WILLOW IGNORED LARKIN'S PLEAS AS SHE TOOK THE STEPS to her room two at a time, slamming and locking the door behind her once she reached her room. Clearing the distance to the balcony door, she pulled it open allowing the raven to waddle inside. Dropping to her knees, she removed the white paper, a smile forming on her face as she read the elegant script. Unable to risk Larkin barging in, she glanced at the locked door before closing her eyes, she concentrated on the memory of seeing her father's severed wings for the first time, the hurt and anger she felt when she watched Mathias walk away with his feeders, as the skin at her wrist turned cold.

Opening her eyes, Willow is shocked to find her mother still lying on the make-shift cot, Zarina sitting in the corner with her head tipped back with the appearance of being asleep.

"What happened?" Willow questioned the room, her focus remaining on her mother's still form. Taking a step, Willow jumped back in shock when a woman who looked exactly like the one in the painting upstairs stepped from the shadows.

"Willow?" Having heard her name a million times, it never sounded sweeter than it did coming from her mother's lips. "Look at you...I never..." Where words failed Cerise, the natural connection between mother and daughter spoke for the pair, making the years which had separated them a mere blip in time.

THADDEUS MADE HIS WAY TO STAND BESIDE ORIFIEL, HIS friend tossing him a quick glance before returning to the beauty of mother and daughter reunited. His throat grew thick with emotion as he watched the pair cling to one another, whispering words only meant for each other.

"I knew your child would be gifted, but I never imagined she would be so beautiful." Thaddeus's complement was half teasing, his way to clear the thick emotion sweltering in the room. "I mean you are hideous to look at."

"Yes, but her mother is gorgeous enough to make even the offspring of an Ogre beautiful."

Thaddeus couldn't argue this fact with his friend. Every Morganti Witch was blessed with features making every goddess in the heavens green with envy.

Willow was the first to pull away, apologizing profusely for saturating her mother's blouse with her tears. Turning in the direction of her father, she caught Thaddeus's smiling face. "That was one heck of a signal you sent."

Uncrossing his arms, "I'm nothing if not thorough."

Thaddeus shifted his attention to Zarina, not liking the pained look in her eyes. There was no time for second guessing or pep-talks of encouragement. This was their moment, the one they'd waited all these years for.

"Well, you scared Larkin half to death." Willow laughed, wiping her remaining tears on the sleeve of her shirt. "How did you know he would take me to the church?"

"Easy," Thaddeus bragged, a sly smile curling up the edge of his lips. "Everything he has stolen from the Factions he's hidden in that church. You're the final piece he needs to collect in order for his plan to work."

Willow nodded in understanding, reaching into her pocket and handing her mother the glass vial she'd kept safe for days.

Cerise wrapped her fingers around her daughter's, swallowing thickly as she chooses her words carefully. "Willow, I know you have used the gift your father gave you to see things from the past. I also know you've chosen Mathias as your mate, a choice I couldn't be happier for."

Willow looked into her mother's eyes, listening to the caution in her voice despite the joy her words conveyed. She waited with bated breath for the but to come, sharing with her yet another piece of the puzzle kept from her.

"However, before you pledge yourself to any of the Factions, I need to show you something. A perspective no one else in the room has knowledge of."

Willow entered the library to the large tables covered in candles. Bowls filled with the herbs they'd crushed surrounded the bottle of Dragons blood at the center of the table, a fresh cut batch of Wolfsbane to the side.

Larkin lay still on the floor, his eyes closed with a pentagram made from salt drawn around him. Saige and Brynn stand on two of the tips, the spell book open on the floor between them.

Stiffening her shoulders, she took her place beside the other Witches. "Is everything ready?"

"Yes," the pair say in unison.

"And you, Larkin. Are you ready?"

Larkin opened his eyes, keeping his focus on the ceiling above him, "Yes."

"Then let's begin."

Saige and Brynn each held out a hand to Willow, taking her place between the points of the pentagram, she completed the circle.

Closing her eyes, Willow pictured in her mind the events her mother shared with her as the two on either side began to chant the words on the page.

A ruffle of wind flipped Willow's hair into her face, the candles flickering around the room. Saige and Brynn noticed, raising their voices as they repeated the chanting several more times. Light from the windows dimmed to non-existent as angry clouds rolled in, intensifying the strength of the wind. Larkin's body jerked as two of the windows shatter, glass raining down coating the room in particles resembling millions of diamonds. Willow bit the inside of her cheek to keep from laughing at a now wide-eyed Larkin, a look of terror etched on his face. A second gust of wind blew the salt from the pentagram into the air, swirling it before dumping it into Larkin's face, slamming the spell book shut and pushing Brynn and Saige onto their backs.

Larkin jumped to his feet, shaking his entire body, sending the salt flying around the room. Willow ducked her head, shielding her face from the salt as Brynn and Saige jumped to their feet.

"Did it work?" Larkin looked from Brynn to Willow, raising his arms in question as the three Witches look to one another.

Pulling herself to her feet, Willow dusted the salt from her clothing, shaking it from the roots of her hair. "Guess we'll find out tomorrow night."

CHAPTER TEN

The sound of jazz filled her ears as Willow breathed in the air of the sultry New Orleans night. Nixx showed up precisely on time, wearing dark sports jacket and matching slacks, offering his arm to Willow to assist her in descending the cement steps. Larkin stayed relatively close to the pair, attempting on more than one occasion to step between them. Willow's eyes lit up the moment she caught sight of the red convertible she'd initially arrived in, turning to a smiling Nixx, his face alive with pride.

"It was finished last night, but I wanted to surprise you. Have you arriving at your party in style."

Not waiting for Willow to reply, Nixx opened the car door, ignoring Larkin and his overzealousness to slide in the car beside her. Once everyone was tucked into the leather of the seats, Nixx turned to Willow as he twisted the key in the ignition, the engine of the antique car purring to life.

"You ready to party, pretty girl?"

Willow answered with a nod of her head and a share of her smile, adjusting the hem of her dress, another borrowed item from the closet across the hall from her room. She would change when the time was right, shifting into something Mathias would appreciate. She watched out of the corner of her eye as Nixx snuck a glance at her bare legs, using the need to roll up her window as an excuse to touch her.

The streets were alive with party goers and spectators appreciating the full moon, which had shifted from creamy white to a dusty pink in its progressive change, fulfilling its notoriety of turning blood red. Larkin barked directions from the back seat, leaving no question on his displeasure of being relegated to the rear of the car.

Nixx pulled alongside the curb, tossing the keys to a sharply dress individual with the characteristics of a Troll. Willow smiled and said hello to the man, much to Larkin's displeasure. Music poured from inside the building, the beat intensifying each time a set of double doors opened to allow a guest to enter. Willow followed behind Larkin as the trio entered the building, surprise clung to her face at the interior. Having only visited the basement, the ground floor was dramatically different with its red and black décor, instead of the intense blue of the hidden floor beneath.

"I would have never guessed it, Willow." Nixx admitted as they stood in line to enter the main room. "A simple girl from Central Florida throwing a shindig like this."

Willow took a hard look around the room, trying to see it from Nixx's perspective. Where he saw fine clothing and beautiful women, she saw Faction members in every shape and size, dressed in borrowed magic and fake smiles.

"Willow didn't throw her own party," Larkin clipped as they crossed the threshold into the main room. "The Factions did this for her."

Putting his hand out to stop her, "Factions? Is that some kind of club you joined?" Nixx questioned, a curious look on his face. Willow had battled with herself on the best way to approach the subject with Nixx, but it was a conversation with her mother that gave her clarity on how best to break the news to him.

"Something like that, I'll fill you in later." Willow called over the music as they approached a rail which ran around the room. Leaning against the thick metal, she took a hard look at the Factions dancing on the floor beneath her. If she chose to accept the legacy of the Morganti Witch, she would rule over the happy faces enjoying the techno music blaring from the speakers all around. Did she want that? Was she ready to be a leader?

"Come on, Willow. You are expected to greet everyone, giving the Faction leaders one last chance to sway you in their direction."

Releasing a long breath, Willow nodded and turned to tell Nixx she would see him in a few minutes. However, she found the space beside her empty and a happy Nixx dancing down the steps, his eyes trained on a group of glamorized Trolls dancing in a circle.

"Your friend has never met a stranger." Larkin tossed his chin at Nixx.

"No, he hasn't." Willow laughed, as Nixx made his way to the center of the circle, the ladies cheering as he removed his jacket, spinning it high in the air as he gyrated his hips.

Larkin reached for her hand, the music changing to another techno song, the lights overhead shifting with the beat. "Are you ready, my love?"

Turning to face him, sliding her hands down his chest, his skin thick and slimy. Willow recalled the first time she'd met Larkin, the handsome face the tea gave him, using the visual to keep herself from getting sick as she stood on her tiptoes. "The question is, Larkin, are you?" Lowering her lips to his chin before she could change her mind, she forces herself to linger there as she rubs her left thigh against his groin.

Faster than she can blink, Larkin swept her into his arms. Jumping over the railing, his wings extended, flying the length of the room and landing with a thud in the center of the stage. The techno music faded as members of a band took their place on the stage. Willow locked eyes with Kiera, the Gargoyle they used as an imposter for Mathias's younger sibling. She was dressed in similar clothing to the last time she'd seen her, the neckline of the beaded gown she wore dipping to the tip of her pelvic bone.

"Oh my gosh, is the band playing for my party?" Willow faked her enthusiasm. Her performance tonight would rival anything these fakes could put out.

"You didn't think the Faction community would throw a party and not have your favorite band play for you, did you?"

Before Willow could answer, a tray of colorful drinks was shoved in her face. "Happy birthday, Willow." Nixx announced before tossing back one of the tiny cups filled with a glowing concoction. Staring at the drinks, she chanted to herself for the liquid to reveal itself. Keeping her poker face intact each cup turned black with dead leaves and several unidentifiable items floating on the top.

"It's not my birthday yet, Nixx." Pointing to the large clock on the wall behind the band. "Sixty minutes to go and then I will gladly let loose."

"Are you serious?" Nixx shouted, a deep scowl marring his face. "An hour ain't shit. Take a fucking shot, Willow."

The smile fell from her face, the atmosphere around them growing thick with tension. Nixx had never spoken to her like that, used those words in her presence ever. It's clear to her those drinks contained the same elixir they'd used to trick her when she first arrived. Taking a glass from the tray, Willow chanted once again, turning the disgusting liquid into colored water, locking eyes with Nixx as she swallowed the contents.

Nixx tipped back his head, shouting in triumph as he

raised the hand not holding the tray into the air. "My best friend is twenty-one, bitches!" Before Willow could stop him, he reached for another cup, tipping the contents back as the group of women he was dancing with earlier, pull him back to the floor, enveloping him like tidal wave.

Larkin slipped his talon around Willow's arm, tugging her toward the steps leading off the stage. "The ritual will begin shortly. Each Faction will have one final opportunity to impress you, giving you their gifts to celebrate your birthday."

Willow stared at the space where Nixx disappeared, an indescribable sadness filling her heart. Allowing Larkin to escort her around the room, she met with various Gargoyles glamorized to look like Witches, Vampires, and Werewolves, each trying to sway her to choose their leader. Kiera, along with the band attempted to play their instruments, however the sound they made reminded Willow they were not the original musicians, and the noise coming out of the speakers gave her the notion to toss a little magic their way, rendering them inoperable. While her Angel magic would be undetectable, she couldn't risk giving Larkin and his followers any reason to suspect her, not when she was so close to ending this.

As the large clock on the wall approached a quarter to midnight, movement at the front of the room captured her attention, pulling her from a boring conversation with a Gargoyle claiming to be a Vampire, requesting the opportunity to design a dress as the one she wore was lacking.

"It's time, Willow." Larkin spoke in her ear, dismissing the remainder of the fake Factions standing in line waiting their turn to visit with her, grabbing her arm and pulling her toward the line of Faction leaders.

Daragis stepped from the line, his massive size blocking the light from the stage behind him, a man Willow doesn't recognize standing beside him.

"Willow, I'd like to introduce my brother."

"Brother? But you boasted about being the last of your kind." Tipping her head to the side, "Is this a new development?"

Daragis shifted his eyes to Larkin and then back to Willow, "Yes, he arrived from Scotland in time for the festivities."

"Scotland? Well that explains it, your family is from Bolivia, at least that's what you told me during our introduction."

Daragis ignored the lie he'd been caught in, or perhaps Zarina was correct in her rationalization; whoever was behind the glamour didn't have the forethought to gain the facts about the Faction members they were impersonating. Turning his attention to Larkin instead.

"I hope my gift to you came in useful." Wagging his eyebrows suggestively at Larkin.

"It did, thank you."

Glancing back at Willow, adjusting his stance. "I do hope you understand it will serve as your birthday gift as well."

Reaching up, placing her open palm against his cheek, tapping the skin three times. "Of course, Daragis, I wouldn't expect anything less." Opening his mouth as if to question her, the reverb from a microphone silenced the music and derailed Daragis's train of thought.

"Good evening, Ladies and Gentlemen." Ophelia stood in the center of the stage, her red dress and matching shawl a direct contrast to her normal bib overalls and dual pigtails. Mel stood beside her, looking even more out of place than she does with his fitted suit. The brass buttons on his jacket reflecting the light overhead.

"Welcome to this monumental occasion where we celebrate the coming of age for one of our own, a young Witch who has finally been returned to us. Rejoining her family in time to bond herself with one of our Factions, their union strengthening the alliance and making our Coven stronger."

Willow bit her tongue to keep from screaming out what a filthy liar Opal was, guilty of stealing her from her mother's arms. She stared hard at the rehearsed smile on both of their faces, waving politely when their gazes collided. Willow pondered how many times Opal practiced her speech before she could say it without showing her forked tongue?

"Faction leaders, can I have you take your places so the selection process can begin?"

The sea of people who'd been dancing to the atrocious music only a moment ago, shifted off the dance floor, creating a border around the edge of the room. The alleged Faction leaders took their place, lining up shoulder to shoulder in front of her. Willow could feel her powers increase with each tick of the clock behind Opal and Mel. As the minute hand fell into place over the number ten, "Willow, it's time for you to begin. Take a final look at each of the Factions before announcing your choice." Pausing for a moment, Willow couldn't help but huff at Opal's choice in words, *your choice* as opposed to the choice of the gods.

Lincoln Devereaux stood directly in front of her, his typical cocky smile alive and well, and polished for the occasion.

"Lincoln," Willow spoke before tipping her head at him.

Running the tip of his thumb across his lower lip, his attempt at seductive eyes fell short with Willow. "Surely you won't hold our little quarrel against me."

"You did call me ugly." Her brows raised in challenge.

Taking two leisurely steps to the right, stopping as she stood before a nervous Daragis. "I spoke no disrespect to you."

"No, Daragis," pointing her index finger to the alleged brother behind him. "But you lied to me, didn't you?"

Daragis tipped his head in confusion as Willow stepped to the side once again, coming to stand before a man she didn't recognize.

"Good evening, Willow. I am Thaddeus Grinwald, you met my sister Patane. She spoke highly of you but fell short in her description of how beautiful you are."

Extending her hand to the Warlock, while keeping her eyes trained on him as he took the offered hand and kissed the back of it, once again holding her tongue despite the overwhelming need to scream at the glamoured Gargoyle. He was an even worse imposter than Lincoln as he looked nothing like the real Thaddeus.

"You and I would be a force to be reckoned with, all of our power combined."

Leaning over, Willow looked to Larkin as she whispered in the fake Warlock's ear. "But according to your sister, it would be a lie, wouldn't it?"

Willow caught the smirk on Larkin's face out of the corner of her eye, gaining one of her own as she imagined the look on his face in a few minutes. Moving to the next Faction leader, another man she didn't recognize, but assumed based on the way he'd dressed and the attitude radiating off him this was the notorious playboy—at least according to his fake sister Kiera—Mathias Priestly. Violet eyes took inventory of her over the rim of dark sunglasses. Long hair, slicked back and gathered in a ponytail at the nape of his neck. The collar of his blue shirt stuck straight up, decorated with several smudges of contrasting lipstick. He was shorter than her Mathias, and his cheeks were absent of the facial hair she loved so much.

"Willow Morganti." His voice was the worst of all, condescending and harsh, not smooth and seductive like the man who held her heart.

"Mathias, I presume?"

Sharing a smirk larger than both Larkin and Lincoln combined, he covered his eyes with his sunglasses as he stepped closer to her. "Kiera said you were hot, but she failed to say you were scorching."

Taking a healthy step back, "Funny, she said you would say anything to win my affections, all the while keeping a harem of women to service you."

The smile fell from the face of the glamoured Gargoyle, as a snicker left Larkin's throat, something Willow would have assumed based on the persona the fake Mathias gave off, would have resulted in a challenge or at least a dirty look. When neither occurred, Willow cast a glance at the clock on the wall and the confident look on Opal's face.

"Have you made your choice, Willow?"

Turning her gaze from the clock on the wall to the sea of spectators surrounding her, not a true and honest face in the crowd. As the last minute of her twentieth year ticked by, Willow's fingers tingled with the magic the stroke of midnight would bring. Scanning memories of the last twenty years filled with nothing special, only to find herself here, in this moment where so much was riding on her decision. Stepping with purpose to the edge of the dance floor, Willow looked to Opal before nodding her head.

"Then tell us dear child, which Faction will it be?" Opal's impatience seeped through her words, giving Willow a needed boost to draw this out for an eternity if she so chooses. As the last five seconds ticked by, the energy from her fingers spread up her arm and into her body, bringing with it a glorious warm sensation like she'd never felt.

Moving to stand before Larkin, the amount of confidence in his face trumped Opal's by miles. Placing her hands on his chest, "I choose…" Dropping her hands, the smile on Larkin's face wavered as she took a step back, remaining silent for as long as she can. "To tell you a story."

"Willow, what are you doing?" Larkin demanded, taking a step toward her.

Holding out her hand, silently telling him to stop, "Patience, Larkin. What I have to say will be of particular importance to you."

She didn't need the clock on the wall to tell her the stroke of midnight had come and gone; she could feel the unmeasurable amount of energy pumping through her veins. Making her way to the center of the dance floor, she caught Nixx's shocked face, sending him a reassuring wink.

"Years ago, long before I was a passing thought, a woman fell in love with the idea of being in love. She was a foolish girl, or so those around her assumed, as she spent most of her days with her head in the clouds, daydreaming."

Willow purposely avoided making eye contact with Larkin

and Opal, directing her words to the hundreds of Gargoyles who followed them.

"One day, this girl heard of a King who wanted to take a wife. Now, in this young lady's time, it was imperative to her survival to have an attachment to a man, and what better man to have than a King? The girl set about formulating a plan, one where she pictured herself arriving at the palace and the King would be helpless to ignore her beauty, taking her as his bride and living happily ever after."

Willow couldn't help but notice how attentive the Gargoyles around her were, hanging on her every word like a group of children at story time.

"However, when she arrived at the palace, she found dozens upon dozens of young ladies who had the same delusion. But this girl held fast, and soon it was her turn to impress the King. Much to her dismay, instead of falling in love, the King bid her a quick goodbye, moving to the next young lady standing in line. As you can imagine, the girl's heart was broken, so much so she fled into the woods where she happened upon a man who asked her why she was upset. Drying her tears, she told him of what happened with the King and how she vowed to never fall in love, living the remainder of her days as an old maid. The man took pity on the girl, helped her off the ground and took her back to his little house deep in the heart of the forest, where he gave her something to eat and drink. Now, this man was no ordinary Good Samaritan. No, this man was what you and I would call a salesman, selling his herbs and elixirs to unsuspecting victims."

With her new magic, Willow could feel the emotion of the crowd changing, once hearts heavy with worry, were now building with curiously.

"He, like the young girl, had an issue with the King for tossing him out of the castle gates, refusing to settle a dispute with another resident of the woods. However, this man's motives for taking in the young girl had nothing to do with her displeasure in the King and everything to do with the fact he knew she was more than a pretty face. The young girl was a Witch, an untamed and quite powerful Witch."

Gasps could be heard all around her, hushed conversations spoken behind carefully placed hands. Larkin stood with his arms crossed over his chest, an impatient expression plastered on his face.

"For years the two lived together, the salesman would go off to sell his wares, or so he told the young woman. She would venture to the castle gates in hopes of capturing the eye of the King. You see, as it turns out, the woman the King chose as his bride never saw her wedding night, her body was found by her hand maids, her throat cut, but the killer was never found. After one such trip to the gates, the woman returned to the little house in the woods to tell the salesman of the King's need for an army, one strong enough to defeat his enemies and keep any future bride safe. The salesman knew how to build such an army, but since he wasn't allowed inside the gates, he had to find a way to get the message to the King. As it happened, during one of his trips, the salesman heard of a powerful Witch who'd been excommunicated for performing black magic. The salesman was no stranger to magic, black or otherwise, having lived in the enchanted forest all his life. In order for his plan to work, he needed to be certain the story of the Witch was true. So, he set off for the village finding not only the Coven, but confirmation the rumor was indeed the truth. He returned to his home and the young woman, with a way to give the King his army and seek revenge on the individual who'd refused to trade with him, resulting in punishment from the King."

Willow glanced at the clock, the hands on the dial telling her she needed to hurry and get to the crescendo of the story if she wanted Larkin to feel the full effect.

"At first, the salesman's plan worked flawlessly; send in the beautiful Witch to seduce and kill the Dragon, and then swoop in and bottle up the blood, keeping what he needed for the spell and selling the rest to the highest bidder. But something went wrong, several somethings actually. The Dragon that was murdered was not just any Dragon. Was he Daragis?"

The fake Daragis looked like a deer caught in headlights, turning to Larkin for the answer. When Larkin's attention remained trained on Willow, the fake Daragis was forced to give the only answer he could.

"I don't know what you're talking about."

"Really?" Willow taunted as more hushed conversations

rippled around the room. "I find that hard to believe, considering it was your father who was killed, whose blood was used to create an army, a very flawed army."

Larkin moved to say something, but Willow was far from finished, holding up her hand to silently caution him. "Your father was not just any Dragon, but one with a bloodline protected by a what was known at the time as the Messengers. By spilling the blood of your father, Daragis, the salesman called down one of their fiercest fighters, his abilities were unfathomable. When he arrived, the Messenger could have struck the salesman down with a single thought, but he didn't. Instead of killing the man, he allowed the blood of the Dragon to do its damage."

Turning about the room, Willow locked gazes with Nixx once again, his attention as rapid as the rest of the crowd. "Now, let's not forget about the young woman who wanted to marry a King." Sticking her finger high in the air, several wide-eyes watched her about the room. "You see, while the salesman was out partnering up with a Witch to do his dirty work, she was able to secure a job within the castle, one that on occasion, placed her in the bed of the King and many of his guards. For some time, she went to him when he requested her, and while her talents in the bedroom didn't impress the King enough to make her his bride, they were enough to gain the admiration of a certain young guard of his. After a while, the guard and the young Witch fell hopelessly in love. Unfortunately for the couple, the guard was part of a contractual obligation to the King, promised to marry his only daughter. So, they kept their relationship a secret, stealing time together when no one was looking, falling further and further in love with each passing year. When the inevitable happened, and the Dragons blood began to take its toll on the army, the young guard sought out his mother, the Witch who'd killed the Dragon and stolen the blood to create the spell. He wanted to introduce her to the young Witch, the woman he wanted to marry, but his mother refused to meet the young girl. She had already sacrificed so much bringing the young man into the world, she wanted to have grandchildren of noble blood and for her son to rule the land around them, instead of struggling to put food on the table like the salesman in the middle of the forest. Too bad she didn't take a moment to meet the young Witch her son was sleeping with. Wouldn't you agree, Nixx?"

CHAPTER ELEVEN

"Enough!" Larkin shouted, the anger in his voice echoing off the rafters in the ceiling, causing many of the spectators to flinch. Willow stood strong, ignoring the poor display of ill-placed testosterone, her eyes locked with the traitorous individual she'd considered family.

Nixx pushed the hands of several women off him as he stepped toward Willow, an amused smile covering his lips, dropping the faux effects of the alcohol he'd made her to believe he'd consumed.

"How'd you figure it out?"

"You first," Willow tossed back, not caring how much of the anger brewing in her chest strangled her words. "Answer my question, do you agree the Witch should have met with the love of her son's life?"

Nixx dropped his eyes to the floor, his pursed lips struggling to hold back a smile. "Not the worst decision of her life." He shrugged, raising his focus back to Willow, his attempt at intimidation wasted on her. "But it's in the top five." Hooking his hands on his hips, tipping his head in her direction. "Now your turn; how the fuck did you figure it out?"

Willow returned his intense stare, showing Nixx in no uncertain terms she wasn't afraid of him. "The night I arrived," shifting her gaze to the couple standing on stage. "Opal gave me a cup of tea, flavored with the single weakness I have, something only two people knew about. Since one of them is dead…" Letting her implication hang in the air, her eyebrow raised for emphasis. "Although coincidental, it gave me reason to question."

A mischievous smile broke out on Willow's face. "Funny thing about your tea, Opal," sharing her smile with the couple who remained on stage. "It only works if you drink it. And for a while I did, but by the time Nixx showed up in my living room, I'd been off the stuff long enough to meet the real Factions. Including the ones, you turned into stone."

Willow's body tingled as the shadows in the room filled with hundreds of familiar eyes, solidifying for her this was what she was destined to do. Turning back to Nixx, "When you arrived with Mel in my living room, you weren't frightened by Saige or Brynn. Having not enjoyed a cup of special tea, any normal human would have run from the room, but not you, Nixx. Not only did you stay, but you told me of your uncle who had the parts for my car. Which would have been generous, except you and I sat on the limb of an old oak tree where you told me you had no family, other than your father. You held my hand and told me we were kindred spirits as you'd lost your mother too."

The cocky look on Nixx's face fell, replaced by darkened eyes alive with fury. "How did you meet the Factions? I would have known if any magic was used."

Willow raised her hand in the air, waving her glowing birthmark high in the air for the room to see. "Not if it was from my father and not my mother. You assumed she'd hidden his magic with hers, but you were wrong. The final kiss he gave me, left behind more than a mark."

"But I would have sensed it when I was beside you, when I touched your wrist."

Willow slowly twisted her head from side to side, her eyes locked with Nixx's. "Clearly, you're not as powerful as you think, Nixx. Or should I call you by your real name…Lymrick?"

As the name drifted off Willow's lips, Cerise and Orifiel stepped from the shadows with their hands intertwined, her necklace secured around her neck and his wings raised high in the air. Willow ignored her parents, keeping her focus on Larkin and Lymrick. Willow thought back to the dress she'd borrowed from the closet across the hall to wear tonight, feeling extremely confident, she allowed her mind to conjure up a dress she knew would send Mathias to his knees, and show everyone in the room just how foolish they'd been to think her ignorant.

"You knew Opal and Saige would betray you even before you struck up a deal with them. When you arrived back at my mother's house after I was born and discovered I was missing, you put feelers out trying to find me. You know, Lymrick, I still remember the day I first saw you, the shy little boy hiding behind the greenhouse in my back yard. You told me your father would be angry if he knew you'd crossed the lake, and for years I kept you a secret."

Orifiel slid in behind his daughter, wrapping a protective arm around her. The dress she'd chosen was far too revealing in his opinion, but in a few minutes, it would no longer be his decision. "A secret which was unwarranted, as Evanora knew who you were. Fairies may have an immunity to Witch magic, but not to mine. When Cerise learned of Ophelia's plans to take us prisoner, I took certain precautions, including giving one of her most loyal Witches a supply of my magic. Something you've been trying to get your hands on for years."

Members of the once frozen Factions began stepping from the shadows, gaining Larkin's attention. Pulling his sword from its sheath and dropping to a defensive stance, as the real Lincoln and Daragis stepped around the glamoured Gargoyles and onto the dance floor.

"How is this possible?" Larkin demanded, holding his stance as if ready for war.

"When my car broke down outside of town, a raven landed on my hood, its eyes a strange blue. Later, when the winds of an incoming storm rousted me from my bed, I found him sitting on the rail, a flier from a local bar clasped in his bill. Lupin, the name of the raven as I now know, continued to bring me the same fliers, which I ignored. During this time, a man with the same shade of eyes came to me in my dreams, filling me with a passion I assumed would only be found there. After meeting with the fake Lincoln, which is when I was given my first taste of my time altering abilities, I learned the man in my dreams was indeed real. It wasn't until an informative and long overdue conversation with my mother, that I learned Lupin is a member of a forgotten Faction, one she struggled to convince to return to New Orleans and rejoin the Council. When Pallen came to her, warning of Ophelia's plans for revenge, Lupin came and offered his services, as he too had the same vision. With the length of time since his people left, both my mother and Lupin were confident he would not be detected, and they were right."

Another shadow progressed into a sharply dressed man, the bright blue of his eyes bringing a smile to Willow's face. Lupin in human form was as handsome as the rest of the Faction leaders, with his dark hair and thick shoulders. Casting a grateful smile in Lupin's direction, Willow turned her attention back to Larkin.

"Unlike you, Lupin was waiting for me with a gift, a handkerchief with a single initial stitched in the corner, a beautiful note addressed to the same name the Blue-Eyed Man from my dreams called me. Not long after that, I neglected to drink the tea you brought me, dumping it down the toilet so I wouldn't hurt your feelings. Having never been sick a day in my life, I had no idea what was happening to me as the effects from the tea wore off, rendering me both ill and giving me the ability to see the magic my mother had left behind in the form of the real door to her bedroom."

Zarina and the two men who accompanied her stepped into the light of the dance floor beside Lupin. Willow couldn't place it, but there was something different about the look of the two silent men, an anger which hadn't been there before.

"I found my mother's books, and her pendant, which I used to leave the house and visit the bar where I met Zarina." Willow turned to Saige who'd been silent since arriving, "You told me Zarina practiced black magic along with my mother. Just like everything else that came out of your mouth, it was a lie."

Saige raised her hand and opened her mouth as if to argue when one of the men beside Zarina stepped forward, extending his hand in Saige's direction and whipping his wrist back and forth several times. "Silence!" he called. "Little Queen speaks the truth and you will listen." With a final stroke of his hand, Saige's lips vanished, her eyes wide as she pulled at the skin covering her face. Willow found herself pleasantly surprised by the sound of his voice, bowing her head at him the moment their gazes collided.

"Black magic was banned from the moment the first Morganti Witch, Josetta, formed a pact with Verin, the then King of the Underworld, allowing his sons to come and choose mates from the Factions. That pact remains in effect to this day." Willow caught Garath nodding his head from the corner of her eye, silently agreeing to continue the arrangement despite her choice in Mathias over him. The conversation with her mother felt as if it had gone on for days, yet was over in the blink of an eye. Garath held a special place in her mother's heart and she was certain Willow would choose the Demon Faction as several past Morganti Witches chose to do.

"But it wasn't until you betrayed me, that I sought Zarina out and learned how deep your deception really was."

Spearing her fingers into the roots of her hair, "My god, Larkin, the children you stole from their parents, the happy couples you separated. For what?" Willow demanded. "Revenge? A better seat at your mother's dinner table?"

Larkin's eyes shifted quickly to Lymrick, as if begging for help. With her patience wearing thin, Willow rounded on Lymrick. "And you. A lifetime of lies, pretending to be something you're not. Playing games with not only my family," waving her arms around the room. "But all of us. You kept secrets, life altering information, just because you could."

Willow's chest heaved with her labored breathing, the air around her thick with the information she'd tossed out. Dropping her gaze to the tops of her shoes, "You assumed I would be fooled by the blood you pulled from the Gargoyle you glamoured to be Daragis. What none of you were aware of, I had the pleasure of meeting the real Dragon leader, gaining a vial of the same bloodline Ophelia was found guilty of stealing by killing Nerus. So, I returned the favor by lying when I said I found my mother's spell book in the solarium. I used a book from the library and filled it with words I found on the back of my shampoo bottle. I used a tiny bit of magic to break the windows and flicker the candles, but the salt in your face," Willow snickered. "That was intentional. A little slap for being such an ass. While Brynn, Saige and myself chanted a bunch of nonsense, my mother and Zarina were directly under our feet, performing the real spell. Using the blood of a Dragon, which was freely given, to set the Factions free of the spell which had imprisoned them."

"I saw you…" Willow began, the pain she'd once felt when she recalled this moment no longer there. "One night, when the temperatures outside dropped and the house was cold, I went into the solarium to close the windows and saw you and Brynn across the street. She was on her knees with your dick in her mouth and in other holes in her body. An impossibility according to you, as you'd been cursed by an evil Witch."

An audible gasp echoed through the speakers in the room, forcing everyone's attention to the stage where Ophelia and Mel stood with horrified looks on their faces. Willow stepped out of her father's embrace. "Bet you're wishing you would have met the love of your son's life now, huh Ophelia?"

Dropping the microphone, Ophelia stepped to the end of the stage, her eyes pleading with Larkin. "Say it isn't true, Larkin? Tell me you haven't been sleeping with Brynn?"

The growing number of Factions forgotten, Larkin

sheathed his sword, returning his attention to Ophelia. "I tried to tell you, but you wouldn't listen. I love her, Mother, and have for a long time."

Willow watched with anticipation as Ophelia slammed her eyes shut before screaming out the words which sent Larkin to his knees. "She's my sister, you fool!"

CHAPTER TWELVE

Despite the circumstances, Willow's gentle nature wouldn't allow her to completely remain indifferent to Larkin's visible pain. While she wouldn't be running to his side to comfort him, she would grant him a moment of reprieve before continuing to unearth the lies she'd uncovered.

"You know, Ophelia, I do believe those are the first words of truth to ever cross your lips."

Willow glanced to her left, as the strong voice of her mother filled the air, capturing not only her attention, but of every eye in the room. "If you care for your son as you claimed you did in front of the King, then tell him the rest before it's too late."

"Too late for what, Cerise?" Ophelia demanded. "Your daughter has already chosen my son."

Willow pushed forward, wriggling out of her father's protection. "I never agreed to accept Larkin as my mate."

Larkin jumped to his feet, spinning on Willow as his wings elongated, his face so close to hers she could feel it ruffle her hair. "Yes, you did."

Unscathed by his methods of intimidation, and no longer concerned with hiding the powers she possessed, Willow raised her hand, the glow from her fingers spreading out and pushing Larkin back several feet, landing him on his ass, feet in the air. "Each and every time I suggested taking you as my mate, you found reason why it was impossible, citing your inability to gain an erection, a flaw you could never burden me with."

Righting himself, "I kissed you—"

"You did more than that to Brynn!" Willow argued, keeping her hand raised and ready. "And yet you have no pledge from her either, something I'm sure Viktor celebrates each and every day."

Murmurs sounded around the room as Larkin scanned the faces in the crowd. "Your relationship with Brynn made you weak, a flaw she couldn't overcome no matter how much she loved you. With her magic gone after her involvement in Nerus's death, she knew it was a matter of time before Ophelia found out she was in love with her nephew, and the severity of how far she'd allowed the relationship to go. With her options limited, she reconnected with several men who'd warmed her bed and given her protection, neither aware of the other."

Shifting her eyes to the stoic Gargoyle to Larkin's right.

"Viktor knew of your relationship with Brynn, but he was ignorant of the many nights she slipped into Mel's bed. The salesman who'd given her shelter and the man Ophelia claimed to be your father."

Larkin lowered his wings, tipping his head to the side as he stared intently at Willow. "What are you talking about?" Not waiting for a reply, he glanced over his shoulder at Ophelia. "What is she talking about?"

Ophelia shook her head, tightening the shawl around her shoulders. "Don't listen to her, Larkin. Morganti Witches will do anything to avoid keeping their word."

Anger bounded in Cerise's veins, the result of Ophelia's words hitting a nerve. Stepping around her daughter, placing herself between Larkin and Willow. "That's right, Ophelia. Go ahead a try to silence the only woman in his life to tell the truth. And for the record, Larkin," pointing her index finger in his direction. "Morganti Witches never, and I mean never, promise something they aren't prepared to carry out. Willow never said she chose you as her mate. She couldn't make such a promise, Larkin, because you aren't a Faction leader." Keeping her focus on an angry Larkin as she posed her next question to Ophelia. "Isn't that right, Opal?"

Willow exerted an incredible amount of restraint as she listened to her mother call Ophelia out, even going so far as to use the abbreviated name she'd been given during their initial meeting. Something told her to remain silent, regardless of how badly she wanted to be the one to deliver the news. So much had been robbed from her parents and while she was certain nothing short of a miracle could make things right, perhaps allowing her mother a voice would continue the healing process.

"You're a lia—"

"Let her finish, Ophelia." Mel interrupted, placing his hand on Opal's shoulder. Willow could see the doubt in his eyes, knowing the truth before it left anyone's lips.

"As Willow said earlier, King Andrew wanted an army, one with incredible power. A few months prior, Ophelia and her sister, Saige, were brought to the Council with charges of using Black Magic in an attempt to create a new Faction. One with all the strengths and none of the weakness of the others. Their experiment resulted in a creature so grotesque and blood thirsty, it killed a village of humans before I could snare it in a trap. I had to call on several other Faction leaders and beg their help in destroying the creature before it could kill anyone else. The use of Black Magic was something which had been forbidden for over a hundred years, during my grandmother's rein. When you arrived at the Coven, asking questions about the Witch who was excommunicated for practicing Black Magic, I was away, spending time with those Faction leaders who'd come to help me. By the time I returned, you and Saige were long gone and gathering the one ingredient you had access to, and she didn't in her prior attempt, Dragon's blood. In order to gain access to where Nerus lived, the pair of you had to cross an area owned by a group of Trolls. When you were detained after being caught trying to sneak across the land without paying, Opal offered herself in exchange for passage." Shifting her gaze back to Larkin. "Nine months to the day later, your aunt, the one you've claimed as the woman you love, helped deliver you, celebrating your lack of taking any of your Troll father's physical features."

Larkin slammed his eyes shut, covering his ears with his claws. "You're a fucking liar!" He roared.

"Am I?" Cerise challenged, stepping forward and signaling Daragis to do the same. "Trolls have one distinct feature no amount of magic can ever get rid of."

Standing before Larkin, Cerise held out her hand, silently demanding Larkin do the same. "My guess is you've never been injured or had a reason to shed even a drop of your blood. Otherwise, your reaction would be so different."

Larkin looked to Opal and then back to Cerise, slowly placing his talon in her palm. "Daragis, if you will do the honors." Without hesitation, Daragis moved his finger diagonally across Larkin's palm, slicing a line with the edge of his fingernail, releasing a thick, orange liquid which glowed like molten lava flowing from an active volcano. Larkin clenched his fist, the orange blood seeping around the edges of his talons, bending in half as a gut-wrenching cry left his throat.

Cerise dropped to her knees, laying a comforting hand on Larkin's shoulder. "I imagine your mother told you horrible stories of how cruel Trolls were, but if you were to ask Willow what she and her father saw, she would tell you a much different story."

"And it would be a lie!" Opal shouted, her face red with fury. "Just as she is lying when she denies agreeing to mate with my son."

"My wife is many things, Ophelia, but a liar isn't one of them, and neither is Willow. But if proof is what you need..." Orifiel drifted off, motioning to Zarina who lay a hand on the man beside her. "The spell on the Faction's is broken. While it's been twenty years, I'm certain Kai's gift would provide all the proof you need."

Willow watched as Ophelia's eyes grew wide, landing on the second silent man who stood beside Zarina, then furiously shook her head. Willow would have to remember to ask her father later what that was all about. Mel dipped his head, dropping to his knee and baring his neck in Willow's direction, before tugging at Ophelia's dress, forcing her to do the same.

"Willow," her father's gentle voice called from the left, a warm hand coming to rest on her shoulder. "It's time to announce your choice, sweetheart."

With a glance at the clock on the wall, the hands showed Willow her father was indeed correct. She could feel the energy in the room change as she thought of Mathias, a new tingle in her body as a rumble filtered through the crowd, the freed Factions outnumbering the Gargoyles who'd followed Mel's lead and dropped to their knees. Garath and Daragis stood sentry at the edge of the dance floor, Lincoln wrapped around a beautiful woman with long dark hair Willow knew without introduction was his mate Rhea. Hushed whispers floated around the room, growing in intensity as Garath and Daragis twisted to the side to reveal the most wonderful sight Willow had ever seen in the intense face of Mathias.

"This isn't possible!" Larkin shouted, severing the moment with his cries. "You swore to me, Lymrick. You said Mathias would die before he saw the light of a new day."

Unwilling to tear her eyes from the man who held her future, Willow ignored Larkin, allowing her body to act on its own accord, reaching out for Mathias as he cleared the distance, his name for her like a prayer on his lips.

"Beauteous."

Willow had no time to reply as Mathias crashed into her body, covering her mouth with his in a kiss so heated her body was instantly on fire. Spearing his fingers in the nape of her neck, Mathias reluctantly separated his mouth from hers, trailing an open mouth kiss to the side of her neck.

"Say it, Beauteous. I need to hear it." Mathias begged as his fangs elongated, venom pooling in his mouth as the essence of her coated his tongue driving him to near madness. He'd never wanted someone as much as he did this beautiful creature.

Knowing what Mathias meant, Willow tipped her head to the side, opened her eyes to find Zeek and Garath holding a feral-looking Larkin by the arms as he struggled to get away from them. Movement to her right pulled her attention to her mother who held Brynn in a glowing blue cloud of magic, her eyes locked on an enraged Larkin who continued to shout it was he who she'd promised to choose. Needing everyone in the room to hear the words Mathias begged for, she looked to the man who'd silenced Saige, motioning with her hand to do the same to Larkin. With a nod of his head in acknowledgment and a single flick of his wrist, the room fell gloriously silent as scales formed along the crease of Larkin's lips.

Without reservation, Willow tipped her head back, exposing her neck as she spoke the words as loud and clear as she could, meaning each syllable with every fiber in her being. "I choose you, Mathias Priestly, to be my mate and eternal love."

Willow felt a warm sensation on her neck and back before her confession had time to leave her lips. She expected to feel a great deal of pain from Mathias's fangs, however none came. Instead, a weightless feeling followed by what she could only describe as the most intense orgasm she'd ever felt, all combined to make her feel as if she were floating and grateful for Mathias's arms around her.

Pulling back, Mathias watched in awe as he took in Willow's face, her bright eyes which could see into his soul, past all of the horrible sins he'd committed, basking in the love he had for her. "I accept you, Willow Morganti, into my Coven as my equal and my heart as my one true love." Returning his lips to hers, he carefully traced his hands down her neck and over her shoulders where he brushed against the set of white wings her birthday and their bond released.

Willow could feel every eye in the room on her, and while

she would love nothing more than to spend an eternity wrapped around Mathias, she knew there were pressing matters which needed to be handled before she gave herself fully to the man taking her breath away with his kisses.

Mathias placed a final kiss to his mate's lips, their stronger bond giving him insight to the thoughts running around her head. She was a born leader, this much he was certain, and he couldn't wait to stand beside her as they turned New Orleans back into the paradise it once was.

Willow searched the crowd as Mathias rounded her body, dragging his fingers along her middle until he wrapped himself around her from behind, placing heated kisses to her exposed neck. "Is this dress for me, Beauteous?"

Retracting her wings, bringing him closer to her. "No, Larkin," she teased, holding back laughter as he sank his fangs into the flesh at her neck once more. She now understood why Mathias couldn't feed from her before, the intensity of the act so great it would take days before she could be parted from him.

Pushing the sensation to the side, Willow's eyes landed on the man who'd silenced Larkin. "I'm sorry, I don't know your name."

The man who she'd seen on a couple of occasions with Zarina turned to face her, bowing his head, several of his dreadlocks falling from his shoulder and into his face. "My name is Arimas, Little Queen."

Ignoring the title, "Thank you, Arimas for helping with Larkin. Is creating skin like that your gift?" Willow pointed at her own mouth, as Arimas took several steps toward her. Mathias removing his fangs from her neck and stepping to her side as if ready to protect her.

Arimas stopped his movements as the room filled with the severe growl coming from Mathias. "It's part of it." He nodded, flashing his eyes between Willow's and a possessive Mathias. "When the curse was placed upon the Factions, Ophelia and Larkin used my power to place the werewolves in the statues you found."

"So, you can alter the makeup of an individual?"

"Yes, but as your father mentioned, it's been many years since we've used our gifts."

"Well, Arimas, how about we dust off your gifts in a little while? I may need your help rectifying a few injustices."

"As you wish, Little Queen."

"Willow, Arimas, just Willow."

With her eyes remaining on Arimas's kind and eager face. "Lymrick, do you recall the night we snuck off to watch the movie you'd waited months to finally come out?"

Lymrick huffed, "Which time, Willow? You and I were constantly sneaking off together."

Before Willow could raise her hand to silence him, her wings sprang from her back and Mathias had Lymrick slammed against the wall, his right hand clamped tightly around his neck as his feet kicked freely several inches from the floor. Lymrick's face turning a deep shade of red as the wall behind him crumbled from the impact, dust and debris raining down around him.

"Don't you dare make it sound as if something happened between us when it didn't!" Willow shouted, the rage Mathias felt transferring to her.

"It's okay, Willow." Her father spoke from behind her, brushing the feathers on her wings in a gentle pattern. "Everyone in this room can smell your virginity. No one is doubting your purity, especially not Mathias."

Willow swallowed hard, her heart pounding in her chest, but left her wings extended. "You know father, I can forgive many things. The night in question with Lymrick involved his illegally obtaining the movie he watched... alone." Willow adding the last part to assure Mathias and as a jab at Lymrick. "I forgave him for stealing without remorse. I've even forgiven him for his involvement in all of this."

Placing her hand on Mathias's shoulder, his body vibrated with the same rage pulsing through her veins. She tried to push him to the side, but Mathias held Lymrick firmly to the wall, the life quickly draining from his face. Using her new power, Willow kissed Mathias, gently whispering against the shell of his ear how she needed him to let go, so she could see his beautiful eyes.

Mathias warred with himself, needing to kill Lymrick for the vile actions he implied about his mate and honoring the request placed on him by the same gorgeous creature.

"Beauteous," he croaked, his voice foreign to his own ears as he released the grip on Lymrick's neck. Turning his face to hers, the light in her eyes brought on a calm he'd never felt before.

Willow kept Lymrick's struggling body in the corner of her eye as she placed her palm on Mathias's cheek, willing him to leave the rage-filled haze and return to her. Placing a gentle kiss to his lips as he blinked rapidly, his new sense of calm doing little to ease the rage inside of her.

Glancing down at the man still struggling for air, "But I cannot forgive him for killing Evanora."

CHAPTER THIRTEEN

Gasps rang out as the accusation fell from Willow's lips. Shocked eyes and gaping mouths hid behind gentle hands as the revelation settled in each ear. Mathias reached out, pulling a tablecloth from a nearby table, wrapping it protectively around his mate. Willow held strong to the mask of strength she'd created for herself, but Mathias could feel the tears she held back, hear the sorrow dripping from her words.

"She was there for me when my mother couldn't be," Willow began, her back teeth clenched in an effort to tap down the emotions rising in her throat. "Shared with me her love of plants and how Mother Nature is to be respected."

"Let me guess?" Lymrick shouted, his voice hoarse from Mathias's attempted strangulation. "Dear old daddy took you on a little outing, bought you ice cream as he showed you the story according to him?"

Dropping her hand from Mathias's face, Willow dipped down, keeping her knees closed as she came face to face with Lymrick. "My father's capabilities are limited to snippets of time, still photographs if you will, of what's already happened. And I suppose one could assume those photographs could be altered."

Waving her hand in the air, the image of the night in question slowly came to life. "But my abilities are different as I can see things as if they are a movie. And for the record, it wasn't my father who helped me see you take Evanora's life, my mother and I had a lengthy conversation. While your trusted guard dog took Brynn to his bed, we used our time wisely."

Mathias and Orifiel stood on either side of Willow as the room watched a battle rage between Lymrick and Evanora, each holding her hand as she held back tears for her fallen guardian. As the final scene played out, showing Lymrick using the power of the lightning illuminating the sky to strike Evanora in the chest, killing her instantly as she refused to allow Lymrick to enter the house.

"I often wondered why neither one of us entered the home of the other, but now it makes sense, you couldn't. Evanora created a spell even your Fairy magic couldn't break, sacrificing her ability to communicate with my mother and the love of her…" Regardless of how short the time Willow's had spent being bonded to Mathias, the emotion of being separated broke through, causing her voice to quake and the room to join her in sorrow. Steadying herself before continuing, "The love of her life, in order to keep me safe so that one day, I could stand here and celebrate the moment you see all of your conniving was for nothing."

Lymrick gazed at Willow for several quiet seconds before tossing his head back in laughter. "You think I didn't plan for something like this to happen? You think I put all of my trust in a bunch of has-been Witches out for revenge?"

Slightly surprised by Lymrick's reaction, Willow remained silent as he pushed off the floor, dusting himself off and rolling up the sleeves of his dress shirt. "I too lived in the same woods as Meldron and Nerus, although back then, my notoriety wasn't what it is today. When I heard about the Council meeting to determine the fate of a pair of Witches who'd used Black Magic, I kept to the trees and made my way to where the Coven lived at the time." Shifting his eyes to Cerise, his shoulders slumped as he took her beautiful features in. "I got my first glimpse of the most gorgeous woman I'd ever seen, Cerise Morganti."

Willow felt a shiver run up her spine at the way Lymrick spoke about her mother, which was quickly extinguished as a growl left her father's chest.

"After the sentencing was over, I rushed back to my place in the forest, readied myself to ask her to consider me as a suitable mate. However, on my way back, I ran into Meldron who was, as usual, having heated sex with one woman, while a second sat by a fire, roasting a dead animal over the flames. I kept to the shadows as the woman by the fire chastised herself as to why the spell didn't work, reciting the ingredients over and over before calling herself stupid and starting over again. As I stood there watching, a single phrase came to me, and before I left the trio alone, I whispered it to the wind who carried it to the Witches ear, Dragons blood."

Willow remained quiet, allowing Lymrick to continue speaking, as for the first time, each word he spoke was the truth.

"When I returned to the Coven, I found Cerise was not there, and none of the other Witches would tell me where she'd gone. So, I returned to my place in the forest, more determined than ever to have Cerise by my side. Several years went by before the wind brought any news of my Cerise, a battle raging at King Andrew's castle. Gathering up my things, I readied to lend a hand, but as I arrived, I caught my precious Cerise in the arms of another, allowing him to do all the things I longed to do to her."

Orifiel smiled slightly, recalling the moment Lymrick spoke of. He'd felt a pair of eyes on them as he and Cerise exchanged their bonds, but he was too lost in her to care.

"I learned of his name, this thief of mates. Orifiel, a Messenger from the Gods, sent down to punish Meldron and the Witches. Instead, he begged the Gods to allow Mother Nature to dish out the punishment when the Dragons blood reached its full potential and allow him to remain on earth, so that he could have my mate." Lymrick spat the last two words out, a belly-full of fury behind them.

"I couldn't watch anymore, so I set off to study the ancient scrolls, to see if my elders had any dealings with this thief, the Messenger. It took a while, but I was able to uncover a passage where another Messenger came to earth but was seduced by a group of Nymphs. He was rendered useless when, in a heat of passion, the group took him to a patch of blooming Wolfsbane, robbing him of his powers and ultimately contributing to his death."

Orifiel kept his eyes trained on Lymrick, all too familiar with the story, although the particulars were somewhat different in his memory.

"I tucked away this information, knowing that someday, I could use it to gain back the love of my Cerise. Many years later, I came across the two Witches, they spoke of having a solid plan for gaining revenge on the Factions, showed me the proof their plan would work. So, I made a deal with the leader, Ophelia, giving her just enough of my Fairy magic to set the plan in motion. In return, she gave me a blood oath. Once Orifiel was out of the picture, she would use her Black magic to make Cerise forget about him, finding love with me instead."

Cerise couldn't hold back as a blast of laughter left her chest, "Black magic doesn't work that way. It steals good magic, killing it and whomever casts the spell."

"I know that!" Lymrick shouted at her, the redness returning to his face. "I may be a simple Fairy to you, but I've seen more Black magic in my years than you can ever imagine. Ophelia, Brynn, and even Saige, all have the same potential to be great Witches, but they lack loyalty, even to each other. Which is why when they shared their plans, I sought out someone close to you, someone you put every ounce of faith into and she betrayed you, just like I knew she would."

Lymrick cast his eyes to Willow. "You speak so highly of Evanora, like she was some kind of goddamned saint. But she betrayed you, Willow. She took you from your mother's arms, because I paid her to, and not out of any loyalty to your parents."

As the disbelief and anger fought for dominance inside Willow's body, a booming voice sounded form behind, capturing everyone's attention, and forcing the color to drain from Lymrick's smug face.

"The Devil is a liar!" Thaddeus proclaimed as he walked to the edge of the railing above the room. "Evanora was many things, but a traitor was most definitely not one of them."

"This is rich, accusations coming from the man I allowed to monitor the Factions, ruling the streets alongside Larkin after he betrayed his alleged best friend." Lymrick tossed, trying his best to conceal the disappointment in his voice.

Walking to the top of the steps, Thaddeus made his way down, stopping briefly to kiss Cerise's cheek. The confidence from earlier returned to Willow, centering her thoughts and illuminating the path she'd laid out before coming here.

"You are indeed correct when you say you befriended

Evanora when you first arrived in New Orleans. But what you didn't know is the meeting was arranged by her clever brother, Pallen, a powerful Warlock from Alabama with one tiny advantage no one spoke of, his ability to foresee the future. When you met Evanora, you were led to believe she was a poor Witch living in the shadow of this great and powerful Coven leader who kept her locked away, doing all the menial tasks while she partied the night away with the leaders of the other Factions. You thought you took this delicate White Witch, with barely enough power to turn the page of a spellbook under your wing, teaching her party tricks and incantations. When in reality, you had a seasoned Red Witch in your presence, with enough power to level the city of New Orleans if she chose to. You promised a life of endless love and more power than the cruel Witch who was her leader, all in exchange for information as you saw fit."

Coming to stand beside Willow, Thaddeus bowed his head and then kissed her cheek, "Fabulous dress, sweetheart. Shows off those glorious wings, your father is undoubtedly proud of." Leaning into her side, his lips brushing the shell of her ear as he attempted to whisper. "And showing those beautiful legs Mathias is dying to climb between."

Willow reached up, brushing a gentle slap against his chest as he turned to Mathias. "Cut the growling, Mathias. No one in their right mind is going to challenge you. Besides, it's annoying."

Thaddeus didn't bother to wait for a rebuttal as he directed his attention back to Lymrick. "As for my role in all of this, you my friend, are as blind to the truth as Ophelia was to the woman her son was fucking." Crossing his arms, Thaddeus adjusted his stance before delivering the information he'd held in for far too long.

"From the moment we learned of Ophelia's plan, we knew she didn't have the power to do it on her own. When word reached us of the relationship between you two, I made it known my loyalty was for sale. When that fated night happened, twenty-one years ago, Zeek and I battled, at least we did a damn good job of making you believe we were, destroying the banister in the house added the perfect touch. Now, I will give it to you, when Larkin ripped Orifiel's wings off you threw us a curve ball, but Evanora paid you back in spades when she failed to check in with you for several years, long enough to strengthen the spell she had over Willow and the house. By the time you arrived, it was too late, your magic was used up after the many spells you assisted Ophelia with. You spent years learning everything you could about Willow, pretending to be her friend, all the while waiting for your magic to return. Out of sheer coincidence, Willow showed signs of her magic the night before you killed Evanora."

Grief wrapped its bony hands around Willow's heart, threatening to take her to her knees once again. A smile and the shake of Thaddeus's head held the tears at bay, the sadness morphing into curiosity.

"What are you laughing at Thaddeus? Is the thought of me killing that wretched old hag, Evanora, humorous to you?"

"No," Thaddeus replied, an eerie calm in his voice.

"He's laughing at the thought of you killing anything larger than a flea." Willow's head whipped in the direction of the angelic voice sounding from the rail surrounding the second-floor balcony. Standing there, wearing a sequined gown and Cheshire grin was a much younger version of her guardian, Evanora. Willow watched in disbelief as the woman made her way along the railing, stepping with grace on the top step as Thaddeus made his way to the bottom of the staircase.

"I saw you lurking in the shadows, like you did every night as Willow readied for bed. Only on this night, I caught the first spark of her father's magic as she was brushing her hair."

Willow tried to recall the night before Evanora died, the memory rushing back of nearly dropping the brush in her hand into the toilet water below.

"She had no clue at the time, just a close-call on a near-miss in dropping something in your hand. But I saw the spark, the sign we'd all been waiting for, so I sent out the signal, disguised in the form of a raging storm."

Lymrick shook his head, convinced the woman before him was an illusion. "How…but…" Watching as the woman who resembled Evanora took the final step, Thaddeus taking her hand and kissing her cheek.

"You allowed your hatred for Orifiel to cloud your better judgement, going to battle with a Red Witch and trying to use her spell against her. I allowed you to believe you'd won when you hit me with the lightning bolt, and you showed me how well our plan was going when you used your magic to glamour a traveler into pretending to be your father and helping to set my body on fire like some Viking. When word got to you of Willow's appearance in New Orleans, you threatened Ophelia if she didn't pull off her end of the bargain, you would end her. Too bad the game was never in your favor to begin with."

Evanora gripped Thaddeus's hand, the confidence she showed to the room a stark contrast to the fear she harbored inside. She'd lied to Willow, allowing her to believe her mother was dead and her father unable to care for her. And now her biggest fear was the beautiful and talented Witch would never forgive her.

"She knows the truth, my love." Thaddeus whispered in her ear, but Evanora needed more assurance, locking watery gazes with Cerise. Squeezing Thaddeus's hand, Evanora cleared the distance, allowing her life-long friend to wrap her in a tight embrace.

"You've sacrificed enough, it's time to be happy."

Willow watched as the two women embraced, the emotion in her throat threatening to choke her. Her body shook as Evanora released her mother, smiling apologetically at her as she cleared the distance between them.

"I'm sorr—"

"You loo—"

The pair spoke over one another, breaking the tension and forcing them both to break into laughter.

"You first, Evanora." Willow offered, holding onto the joy the brief laughter left behind.

Taking a deep breath, Evanora opened her arms, inviting Willow into a hug. "I'm so sorry to have kept you from your parents."

Willow allowed the tears to flow as she stepped into her guardian's embrace. "I saw everything. It is I who am sorry for keeping you from Thaddeus." Pulling back, "Look at how beautiful you are, Evanora. That was quite some magic you used to make yourself appear old." Willow perused her guardian's appearance, gone were the baggy clothing and silver hair, replaced by a form fitting dress and raven hair. Even her complexion, which once housed a multitude of wrinkles and age spots, was now peaches and cream with the same youthful glow she saw in the mirror each morning on her own face.

"It's the same magic that flows in your veins." Casting a look over Willow's shoulder. "You made the right choice, Willow. But it's time to take Mathias out of here, the bonding process is much harder on males."

Willow shifted her attention to Mathias standing behind her, noticing his face contorting as if in pain. "Go ahead, Sweetheart," her mother whispered. "Arimas will make sure all the guilty parties remain in the room until sentencing can be carried out."

CHAPTER FOURTEEN

Mathias wasted little time as he wrapped his arms around Willow, sending Orifiel a look which conveyed his promise of taking good care of his only daughter. He couldn't wait to stand in the fresh air, free of Ophelia's spell as he professed his love to Willow in front of the entire Faction community. First, he would need to complete the bonding ritual, taking Willow's virginity and claiming it. For the first time in his long life, he was both eager and terrified, knowing he need to inflict pain on the woman his instincts swore to protect.

Shooting one final glance at Larkin, Mathias found it impossible not to gloat, celebrating in the obvious defeat written all over his face. "You lose again, Larkin." The words were out of Mathias's mouth before he could contain them, yet he didn't regret them, and wouldn't have pulled them back if he could.

Dropping his eyes to Willow, he scooped her up, moving at inhuman speed as he leaped from the crowded dance floor to the railing of the second-floor balcony and out the front door. After the spell had been broken the night before, Mathias, along with several members of his Faction, went to his home inside the Quarter, preparing it for Willow's arrival. He wasn't foolish enough to believe several of the other Faction leaders didn't do the same, as Morganti Witches have a history of choosing the Demon Faction. Holding Willow close as he pushed his car to its limits, he was never so grateful this one had broken tradition.

Willow wished they could take a moment so she could explore the Quarter, but Evanora was right, she could feel Mathias's body vibrating from the effects of the bonding. Her understanding from what her mother explained, there was a war going on inside of him, a man splitting in half, one side demanding to complete the ritual, while the other was desperate to protect her.

"Mathias," Willow called softly, needing to ease some of the tension coiling him like a vice. "Since it's my birthday, and I was never allowed to leave the house, would you do me the honor of escorting me through the Quarter later this evening?"

Willow felt the muscles in Mathias's leg contract as he pressed the gas pedal to the floor. "You've been to the Quarter, Blood M—"

"No, Mathias. I want to walk the streets, dance behind the bands, celebrate like all those people I watched from the balcony when Larkin wasn't looking." It was a cheap shot on her part, having seen the exchange of testosterone between the two men, and wanting to know what Mathias meant with his departing comment to Larkin.

Mathias focused on the turmoil inside his body in order to hide the smile tugging at his lips. Cerise made it abundantly clear to everyone there was to be a great celebration following the Council trial to ring in the new queen and make up for all of the birthdays Willow had missed. Orifiel wanted, as Alaric had done when Mathias took over, to retire for a few years with his mate, reconnecting without all the Faction business getting in the way.

"You're right, Beauteous. As a vampire of over three-hundred years, I forget the anticipation of a twenty-first birthday. If it is your wish to experience the Quarter, nothing would please me more than to see the city I love through your eyes."

Pleased with his response, Willow leaned over, placing a kiss to the edge of Mathias's jaw, his reaction by way of a deep growl reminded her of the second question. "What's with the animosity between you and Larkin? And don't say it's because of his touching me," Willow warned. "I may be much younger than you, but I know deep-rooted anger when I see it."

Whipping the wheel to the right, wishing he'd built his home much closer to the center of the Quarter. There was no room in his relationship with Willow for secrets, especially after everything had been revealed and the bad guys labeled.

"When your mother put the call out for help from the

other Factions, Alaric, my Coven leader at the time, pulled us from—" Mathias abruptly stopped, recalling the handful of women he was enjoying in a village not far from the castle. While he wasn't the same man he was back then, reminding Willow of the man-whore he used to be wasn't favorable.

"Hey, don't dilute your words for me, that part of you is in the past. Granted, it's not my favorite, but I'm dealing."

Just when Mathias felt as if his heart was full, this precious creature exhibited such grace which made him love her even more. "Pulled us from a long overdue feeding. Kieran of course exercised his displeasure." Mathias huffed, his wish for his youngest brother to find the kind of love he had, showing him not all women are full of hate.

"I've seen Kieran in action, so I'm not surprised he didn't want to leave." Willow added, running her nose along the edge of Mathias's jaw, soaking up the intense scent of him there.

"It's more than food for my brother," Mathias started, as he ignored the changing traffic light and the blare of several horns from startled drivers. "Once he discovered his love for music, he spent nearly as much time perfecting it as he did enjoying the spoils of being a vampire. After the band was formed and gained some notoriety, a group of bible-thumping protesters made Devils Revenge the subject of their mission statement, popping up at different venues with their vile signs and words of hate."

Willow shifted closer to Mathias as he sped through a

second red light. "Surely he's gotten over it. This was what…thirty years ago? Those protesters have grown up and gotten lives by now."

"One would assume; however, this particular group has passed the torch so to speak, the new generation just as passionate about delivering their message of hate. Imagine going from thousands of people enjoying your music to a group surrounding your tour bus, demanding you return to the depths of hell you came from."

Willow recalled reading an article from the late sixties of one such protest. The woman interviewed claimed to be on a mission from God, ridding the world of the satanic trash the band promoted. "Guess he's glad he doesn't have to deal with that anymore, since the band has been silent for several years."

"Band wasn't silent. They've just run with a few well-placed rumors about some personal issues."

Willow recalled the radio announcer's message to Kieran, something about heavy is the head who wears the crown.

"Kieran continued to make music from his room inside the sewers, gearing up for one of their transitions where the son takes over for the father. With our inability to age, over the years they've had to fake a few deaths, affairs with invented people which produced musical prodigies who looked and played exactly like the original members. A few well-placed memory spells and the record label was none the wiser."

Willow could sense there was something more, "And?" She prodded, needing both the distraction from the way his hand felt between her legs as he shifted gears and to learn the correlation between Kieran's band and the animosity between Larkin and Mathias.

"And it was the same village where Kieran met Sierra, a Witch he fell instantly in love with, but whose father refused to allow the couple to be together, despite every indication they were a mated pair. During the battle where Ophelia gave Larkin the last of the elixir, your mother promised Kieran when the fight was over and the Factions were living in harmony, she would approach Sierra's father and convince him to allow the mating bond to continue. When Larkin barricaded the door with his new and improved body, it was␣Kieran and I who were able to break it down. We found him practically celebrating in the middle of the room, the blood of the King's daughter all over his hands. Kieran got to him first, slamming him into a wall while I checked on the girl, who was a few breaths short of death. Larkin began spouting off how we were too late about a second before I sank my fangs into the girl's neck, giving her enough of my venom to change her into a Vampire. After we destroyed Ophelia's army, Larkin vowed he would get revenge for stealing the girl away from him. Your mother made good on her promise and brought Sierra back to camp before taking off with your father."

Confused, Willow gripped the arm Mathias had between her legs. "Wait, the princess lived? According to Zarina, the princess was killed by Larkin."

Turning the final corner, his home now in sight. "She's right. The princess, Verona, did die, but not in the dungeon and not by Larkin's hand."

Turning to face Mathias as he cut the engine. "Then how, Vampires are immortal?"

Taking her face between his palms, drinking in the deep pools of her eyes. "One last discussion about Larkin and we leave him, and the rest of the Factions, outside for the rest of the night, deal?"

"Deal," Willow agreed eagerly, turning her head slightly to capture Mathias's thumb between her lips.

"Sierra and Verona became close friends considering the amount of time they spent together. After we moved to New Orleans, Sierra and Verona took care of all the needs for the band, including glamouring people and creating fake stories to explain the changes in members. On the night of your birth, while Kieran and I were doing our part in your parents' abduction, Verona and Sierra were supposed to wait for us inside the sewers."

Mathias dropped his gaze, the same anger building in his chest as the day it happened. "Sierra wanted ice cream, so they took a detour. Brynn and Viktor were waiting for them once they reached the entrance to the sewers. By then the curse was in full force, Verona couldn't see, and Sierra's magic was gone. Brynn had a vendetta against Verona for stealing Larkin's attention, so Viktor helped her tie her up and hang her from the ceiling of the church where she was left to die. Sierra was rendered defenseless, and Brynn used Viktor's sword to behead her, the only way to kill an Immortal Witch."

Willow's heart ached for Kieran, she couldn't imagine losing Mathias and their bond hadn't been completed. "Did you and Verona…?"

Mathias shook his head, "She was a pain in my ass from the moment I turned her. But she was loyal, and that goes a long way with me. Kieran has spent the last twenty years writing his ass off trying to forget her. I expect now that we can walk around above ground, he will go on tour again soon. It's what he does when he needs to hide from something."

Willow couldn't put her finger on it, and maybe it was the fact she'd spend a limited amount of time with Kieran, but the way he acted the last time she saw him wasn't of a tortured soul. Perhaps she could talk with him once the trials were over, before she could think of him any further Mathias rounded the car, pulling her from the seat, tossed her over his shoulder and sprinted into the house.

Mathias used every ounce of self-control as he laid his new mate on the comforter of his bed, their bed. While Willow was half Angel and likely possessed at least half the strength he did, there would be no chances taken.

She'd driven him mad when he walked into the room, her dress exposing her slender legs and bare shoulders. While he appreciated her beautiful body, he could tell by the musk hanging in the air the majority of the men in the room had as well.

Kissing down her supple neck, tracing his tongue over the still visible bite marks from earlier, he was rewarded when a deep moan left Willow's throat, putting a smile on his face and increasing his already stiff cock. He'd had countless women under him like this, but none of them, not even the most seasoned of his Feeders, made him feel this incredible.

He was granted with a second moan following by a quick gasp as he placed open mouthed kisses along her collarbones. Her body arched as his tongue lapped at the space between her tits, kneading those perfect globes in his hands as Willow began to purr. Pressing his leg between her thighs, Mathias could feel the heat from her core, the slight dampness of her arousal when he ground his thigh into her cloth-covered pussy.

"I can smell you, Beauteous. Feel how much you want me."

Willow was too lost in Mathias's skilled touch to form a coherent answer, granting him a few nods of her head as she raised her hands above her head, the fabric of her dress slipping down and exposing her breasts. Lying on her back, she thought of how she should be embarrassed to be half naked before a man she'd spent most of their interactions were in dreams, crossed her mind. Those thoughts were quickly forgotten as she waved her hand in the air, rendering the pair of them naked as the day they were born.

Mathias chuckled at his mate's voracity, having assumed based on her virginal status he would have to work hard at getting her comfortable with being naked with the lights on. He'd never been so thrilled at being wrong.

Separating her legs, allowing her knees to fall to the side, "Touch me, Mathias." Her request out before her inner shy girl could argue. "I want the dream to be real."

Searching his memory, at first Mathias was confused as to what she meant, until he recalled one of the first times he invaded her dreams. When Thaddeus came into the sewers to let him know of Evanora's signal, he'd brought Luprin with him. With a drop of his blood and piece of the cording holding his crucifix, Luprin swore he would help Willow find her way to the Factions. Kissing down Willow's soft abdomen, he remembered the first time he saw her through Luprin's eyes, the fierce young lady who tried desperately to save a bird from the jaws of an angry wolf. How many nights he'd sat beside her, watching as she stared longingly at the New Orleans street below, desperate to be a part of the party instead of a spectator.

Running the tip of his nose along the top of her mound he recalled with perfect clarity the first time he was pulled into her dreams. Lupin warned him this could happen but advised him not to take things too far and temp the God's to change their minds. Mathias took the warning to heart, having committed enough crimes in his immortal life, he wouldn't risk losing the one thing he craved more than blood.

"Like this, Beauteous?" Mathias questioned before diving his tongue deep into her heated core, separating her lower lips with his thumbs as he nearly came from the taste of her essence. Just as in the dream, he kept his eyes locked with hers, pushing his tongue in and out of her at blurring speed.

"Yes," Willow admitted through labored breathing, the feel of his tongue and fingers so much more intense than in her dreams. She could feel the wave building, the delicious burn in the bottom of her belly. But it was the moment when he removed his tongue from inside of her, clamping his mouth around her clit and sucking hard, which sent her screaming over the edge.

Mathias wanted to drink every drop of her orgasm, covering his entire body with her essence, but he knew this was the optimal time to sheath himself inside of her, breaking her maidenhood with the least amount of pain inflicted. Ignoring his own needs, Mathias leaned back on his heels, gripping Willow's hips and sliding her body toward him. With her skin glowing from the layer of sweat her orgasm created, he leaned over, running his tongue from the underside of her right breast, across the harden peak of her nipple. Closing his eyes as he savored her salty taste on his tongue, filing it away in his deepest memory before uttering the words which had burned on his lips since he first laid eyes on her.

"I love you, Willow."

Willow's mind was too clouded in climax-haze to register what was happening before she felt Mathias line himself up to her entrance, slipping deep inside her. Based on what she'd read and the small details she'd managed to gather from the women in her life, she expected to feel an enormous amount of pain when he broke through her barrier. While it did sting enough to make her muscles contract, the oddest sensation filled her body bring a soothing warmth, coaxing her wings to spread out beneath her.

"I...oh, God!" Mathias roared above her, his eyes slammed shut and mouth gaping, the sensation increasing with each thrust of his pelvis, his crucifix rocking back and forth like a pendulum. Willow could feel his cock growing inside of her, hitting a place deep within making her toes curl each time he rubbed across it. Acting on instinct, Willow reached up, gripping Mathias by the shoulders and flipping them over, gaining a new angle and allowing her to keep him where she needed him.

Mathias would have smiled at his mate's tenacity, but the euphoria of being buried inside her was too much to focus on anything else. He could feel the beginning of his own orgasm hovering in the distance, trying his best to hold it at bay until he could fulfill her needs. Sex had never been like this for him, historically there was only one motive on his mind, get his and move on. This time was different, it was more than just an act which accompanied his need for blood, this was his forever.

"Mathias!" Willow called, the tingling in her belly felt so far off, no matter how fast her strokes were or how hard she met his pelvis with hers, the crash she craved would not come to her. Reaching down, she pressed her index finger against her swollen clit, rubbing the sensitive flesh back and forth as Mathias had done with his mouth, feeling assured of the same outcome if she remained persistent in her strokes.

The battle to hold back his orgasm was about to come to a disastrous end as Mathias watched Willow pleasuring herself while riding him. Venom pooled in his mouth, his hunger for a taste of her blood overruling the growing need of his cock. Without thought, Mathias pulled Willow's fingers from between her legs, shoving the glistening digits in his mouth. It wasn't enough, as the musky taste of her did little to cool his growing need to taste the deepest part of her. Flipping her hand, Mathias locked eyes with his mate as he sank his fangs into the flesh at her wrist. Mathias felt Willow's walls milking him and the joint cry of each other's names, seconds before everything in his world faded to black.

CHAPTER FIFTEEN

"I'd give anything to have seen your face." Kieran teased Mathias as the pair watched Willow blow out the candles on her birthday cake. He'd grown a strange fondness for his new sister-in-law, despite the recent addition she'd gifted his brother.

"Of that I have no doubt," Mathias tossed back. "Thankfully, my mate is as intelligent as she is beautiful." When the light returned to Mathias, he'd found the faces of Orifiel and Zarina staring down at him and a worried looking Willow being held tightly by her mother.

"A fucking heartbeat!" Kieran exclaimed, gaining the attention of a table of Trolls celebrating across the aisle. "Better you than me, Mathias. I wouldn't know what the fuck to do if my heart began beating again."

Mathias tipped his glass of scotch at the Trolls in apology before returning his attention to Willow who was licking frosting off her fingers, his cock twitching at the thought of her doing the same to his aching appendage.

"Yes, you would, Kieran. You're just not ready to admit it."

"A beating heart would indicate I'm alive, and we both know I've been dead for a long time." Kieran argued, tipping back the bottle of Jack Daniels as he watched a female vampire dancing by herself. Sierra had been the best part of him, and she'd been ripped away before he was able to tell her how much he loved her.

"Having a beating heart doesn't mean you're alive, plenty of human's have perfectly working ones and haven't lived a day in their life."

After Zarina checked him over and ruled out the possibility of any new curses, she and Cerise hit the ancient scrolls in an attempt to find out why Mathias's heart began to beat after biting Willow. It didn't take long for them to come back with a story of a Werewolf who was given Angel blood when something went wrong in the middle of a shift, leaving him half man and half wolf. When Mathias latched on to Willow's wrist, his fangs landed in the center of her birthmark, giving him not only a healthy dose of her Angel blood, but enough Angel magic to restart his heart. Willow remained on the edge of tears until it was proven his vampire abilities remained. Once Zarina deemed Mathias right as rain, everyone cleared out, allowing Mathias to take his new mate back to bed where he loved her well into the early evening.

Slamming the bottle on the table, Kieran turned to Mathias. "Be that as it may, I'll pass on the whole beating heart thing. Mine shattered the day Sierra took her last breath. Besides, I leave on tour in a month, got no room deal with any new bullshit." Standing from the table, he stalked over to the group of female vampires, laying his arms over the first two he came to and proceeded to escort the group of them out the door.

A plan formed inside Willow's head as she watched Kieran toss back whiskey and leave with a handful of women, the pain of his past etched on his handsome face. She could fix this. Her mother showed her which spell to use after Kai gave her a demonstration of his abilities, to see through and replicate even the most complex magic, bringing the truth out of even the most seasoned liar. Which, she surmised, was the reason Ophelia wanted nothing to do with him.

"Everything okay, Birthday Girl?" Willow turned slowly toward her mother's smiling face, basking in the warmth she provided just from being near her.

"It is now." Returning her attention to the back of Kieran as he stepped out into the busy New Orleans street. Cerise followed her daughter's gaze, happy to see the Morganti legacy would be carried on.

"Good," wrapping her arm around Willow's shoulders. "It's time for presents."

The table which housed her massive cake has been cleared of the delicious confection, a vase of roses and several small bow covered boxes beside it. Standing around the circular table were the leaders from each Faction, her own personal slice of heaven positioned at the end.

"With your mating ritual complete and this being the night of your twenty-first birthday, the other leaders, and myself, have collectively agreed a celebration such as this deserves a spectacular gift." Lincoln waved his hand over the top of the gifts, as the others nodded their heads in unison. All except Mathias, who looked oddly nervous.

A hand to Willow's shoulder caught her attention as Orifiel placed a chair beside her, gifting his daughter a smile as he helped her take a seat.

"With the need to always be first in our blood, we drew straws to see who would start. Naturally, Daragis cheated," Lincoln teased as the room filled with laughter. "But we are all men of honor and have allowed him to steal this victory and add it to his treasure chest."

Daragis stepped around the table, deliberately hip-checking Lincoln as he reached for the gold box, gaining a slap on the back and another round of laughter from the crowd.

"It's true, Dragons have been labeled thieves, but only because they are more handsome than werewolves and have more beautiful mates."

Willow laughed and clapped along with the rest of the room, enjoying the friendly competitiveness between the men.

"As you know, my father was killed for his blood, a gift he would have given freely if Ophelia would have asked. Nerus was a great man, one who showed me, and my brothers, what it is to treasure something in the way he cared for my mother." Willow watched with a lump in her throat as Daragis opened the box, handing her a tiny bracelet, a single bead dangling from the end.

"The gold is from Egypt, some of the finest in the world. The jewels are a combination of rubies and emeralds, known to be valuable to every good Witch. The bead at the end contains a drop of my blood. Something, just like my father, I will always give freely."

Willow stood from her chair, the tears she held at bay now freely rolling down her cheeks as she wrapped her arms around Daragis's neck. "I will wear it always," she swore through the thick emotion, before placing a gentle kiss to his cheek.

Taking her seat, Willow allowed her mother to fasten the bracelet around her wrist, avoiding the arm with her birthmark.

After Willow opened her eyes from the most intense orgasm of her life, her heart shattered when she found Mathias unresponsive. Once he woke and it was discovered how powerful her birthmark was, she was tempted to wrap something around it, but Mathias convinced her it wasn't necessary.

Azdren, the leader of the Pride Faction, moved forward, taking a deep green box from the table. Having little interaction with him despite everything that happened, Willow hoped to strengthen the relationship, making the Pride more active in the Council.

"I haven't had the same opportunity as the other Factions to get to know you, however I do hope you will accept my gift and the open invitation to visit our lands and see our people and our way of life." Willow appreciated the deepness of his voice, and the wildness of his hair which gave him a certain edge.

"Of course, I would love to come and meet everyone. I do, however, hope to convince you to take an active role in the Council."

"Anything you wish, Willow. You've sacrificed enough for the Factions, it's time we repay the debt." Azdren pulled a silver ball from the box, resting it in the center of his palm and offering it to Willow. "This ball has been in my family for hundreds of years. It's said the holder will have the power to gain entrance into our minds, communicating with the Pride even from a long distance." Azdren placed the ball in Willow's hand, folding his fingers around hers. "Keep it safe and use it anytime you need to speak to one of us, no matter the time of day."

Willow was overcome with the significance of the gift, having access to their thoughts required a huge amount of trust. "I will guard it with my life." Holding the ball to her chest as she bowed her head and Azdren returned to his place in line.

"Sorry, Willow, but Rhea already owns my balls," Lincoln

teased, sending a wink at Azdren as he passed him. Rhea mockingly tapped the side of her purse, sending a wink in Lincoln's direction. Instead of picking up one of the boxes on the table, Lincoln reached around his neck, removing a silver chain and placing it around Willow's neck, kissing her cheek as he pulled away. "This is a moon stone, given to me when I won the challenge for Alpha. According to my great-grandmother, this is a piece of the moon from the night I was born, although in truth it's probably a chunk of a meteor which fell to Earth, but I'd never argue with my granny."

Willow appreciated Lincoln's humor, clearing the tears from her eyes and allowing her to enjoy the moment.

"Tell your granny I love it, and will keep it close to my heart."

Lincoln was pushed to the side as an eager Garath took his place, the next to the last box in his hand. "Move over, Lincoln. Everyone knows you would talk all night if we didn't cut you off." Willow was too happy to be shocked by their playful nature. Garath opened the box, taking Willow's hand and laying what looked like a key made of glass in the center of her palm. "I would wager most of the Factions assumed you would choose me, given the history of our two families. I find myself equally grateful and saddened by your choice."

Garath's voice cracked as he lowered his gaze to the crystal key. "While I'm grateful my friend Mathias has found his equal…" he trailed off. "I received word from my brother, the woman I hoped to mate with did not wait for me as she promised. Instead finding comfort in the arms of one of the guards assigned to protect her in my absence."

Wrapping her hands around Gareth's, her plans for the Factions expanding. "Do not lose faith, Garath. Your mate is out there; you just haven't found her yet."

Nodding his head, "This is the key to the Underworld, one of three in existence. We owe you everything, Willow. But this is my most prized possession and I know of no other I would trust with keeping it."

A commotion at the entrance to the bar gained everyone's attention, stilling the words on Willow's lips of not wanting to take his only key.

"This is a private party; your kind isn't welcome!" One of the Trolls who stood sentry at the entrance shouted at someone much smaller, as Willow couldn't see anyone.

"We don't want any trouble. Only to speak with the Morganti Witch who defeated Lymrick."

Willow didn't recognize the female voice, however by the way her father dashed across the room he certainly had. Mathias rounded the table, taking her into his protective embrace as Orifiel spoke in hushed words to whomever was at the door. "Can you see who my father is talking to?" Willow questioned, unable to see despite standing on her tiptoes. Before Mathias can answer, Orifiel says something to the Troll, placing what Willow assumes is a friendly pat to his shoulder before turning in her direction, revealing the shortest woman she'd ever seen. Mathias's grip on her increased as the two made their way across the floor, a low rumble spreading like a wave through the air as Factions spoke behind hidden lips.

"Willow, this is Arcadia, a representative of the Fairy Faction who has come to plead for her people."

Shifting her eyes from the face of her father to the dark-haired woman who stood before her. Willow could sense the nervousness coming from her, rivaling her own. With a deep breath, she stepped away from Mathias, extending her hand in greeting. "Pleasure to meet you, Arcadia. How can we help you?" Willow purposely added the *we* as technically her mother was still queen.

"Word came today on the wind of your triumph over Lymrick. This is great news for my people for many seasons. He has ruled by terror, forgetting the laws our elders placed in the ancient scrolls and sacrificed many of our resources for his personal gain. I was chosen as the new leader of the Fairy Faction, and come today to beg you not to hold my people responsible for his crimes against you."

No one had to tell Willow how important her response would be. How every eye, including her mother's, was fixed on her, waiting for a decision which could shape the opinion of everyone in attendance.

"While I commend your bravery in coming here, you must know based on recent events the reputation of the Fairy Faction has been significantly damaged."

Willow watched as Arcadia swallowed hard, adjusting her stance while keeping her head high and emotions in check. "You're correct—"

"I wasn't finished," Willow's tone was heavy and authoritative, earning a hint of a smile from her mother.

"It's my belief the sins of the father should not stain the hands of the son, or in your case, daughter. I am, however, not naïve enough to trust the word of a complete stranger, regardless of how noble they present themselves. I will honor your appointment as Faction leader, but with the stipulation the Fairy's will be monitored for the period of five years for even the slightest amount of dishonesty against the Council. If none is found, you and your people will be allowed to return to your Council seat and regain the right to vote on Faction matters."

Arcadia dipped her head in respect. "You have my word the Fairy Faction will not forget your mercy and will not disgrace ourselves by going against the Council." Willow shot her gaze to where Kai stood, her eyes silently asking him if the Fairy was telling the truth. With a quick nod from Kai, she turned her attention back to Arcadia.

"I also offer my apology for my lack of gift for your birthday. You have my assurance I will correct the error immediately."

"Do not feel obligated to give me a gift, I have everything I could possibly want and more."

Arcadia dropped her chin slightly, not enough to catch

anyone's attention, except for Willow's. "However, I do expect you to represent your Faction and prove yourself trustworthy tomorrow morning during the Council sentencing for Lymrick and the others."

Dipping her head once again, "It will be my honor." She said as she kept her eyes on Willow and backed out of the room into the night.

When the door to the bar closed, it was as if someone pressed play on the party, conversations began again as Mathias took several steps toward the table, picking up the remaining box. Turning to face Willow, "I'm not sure if I can top that, coming here alone after what Lymrick did took a great amount of courage."

The fact that Mathias's hands were shaking didn't get past Willow, or how he'd taken several deep breaths since walking away from her. She wanted to blame all the oddities on his newly beating heart, but the connection which buzzed between them told her it was pure nerves.

"But I'm going to try."

Mathias took the pouch from the box, tossing the cardboard onto the table. When Willow stepped into the shower before coming out for her birthday, he'd made two phone calls; one to Orifiel and the other to the Faction Concierge with instructions to go into his private safe and retrieve something for him.

"As cheesy as this sounds, Willow, I loved you before long before I met you. Always knowing even as a boy, you were out there waiting for me. Thankfully the Gods saw fit to have me changed into a vampire so I would have the opportunity to spend forever with you."

Mathias took several deliberate steps in Willow's direction, slipping his shaking fingers into the black pouch in his hands. "In the eyes of the Council and every Faction, you and I are fully mated, a bond I don't ever want to break. But you've spent your entire life in the human world where there is a little more to taking a partner than accepting the God's decision. I want every creature, Faction or human to know you're mine."

With his new heart pounding away in his chest, Mathias dropped to one knee before the reason for his existence. "Willow, will you marry me?"

CHAPTER SIXTEEN

Willow studied the familiar faces as members of each Faction took their seats in the theater-like room. Mathias and the other Faction leaders sat at long, mahogany table at the base of the seats, their banter from the night before continuing despite the seriousness of the moment.

What felt like a million butterflies danced in her stomach, the gentle touch of her mother's hand on hers doing little to calm her unease. According to what she'd been told earlier, the Council meeting would begin with Cerise resigning her position and asking the Factions for any nominations to the position. Once everyone had the opportunity to add their candidate, a vote would be taken and a new Queen crowned, with the first order of business the sentencing of the parties involved.

Casting her gaze to Mathias, wishing she could have sat beside him instead of up on the platform with her mother.

Mathias shot her a wink, accompanied with a mouthed *I love you*. Willow returned the gesture as she spun his ring on her finger. The decision to marry Mathias came easy, convincing him to wait until things settled down, not so much. In the end, and after numerous acts of seduction, he agreed to her terms of waiting.

As the last of the Factions came into the room, the Troll who attempted to stop Arcadia from entering the bar walked over to her mother, whispering something in her ear then scurried to the back of the room. Willow watched with the eyes of an eager student, needing to know how to properly command a room, on the off chance the Faction vote went her way.

With the grace of seasoned ruler, Cerise stood from her chair and called the meeting to order.

What felt like an eternity later, Willow stood in the center of the platform, the Factions below clapping and chanting her name. Zarina used a bundle of burning sage to bless the new Queen and the reformed Council. The vote had been unanimous, and no other candidates were proposed.

"Thank you, everyone. I promise to do my best to be a fair and just leader." Willow announced to the crowd, her eyes landing on each leader and then to the hundreds of members of the Paranormal community. She could do this, with the help of the Council and those closest her, she would rebuild this city and strengthen the Factions. But first, she had to remove the diseased and rotting parts, before building on a new foundation.

"Guards, please escort the accused into the room."

Willow expected the accused to shuffle in with shackles and chains binding their wrist and ankles, much like the way the Gargoyles escorted the Troll into her mother's house. The reality, however, shouldn't have surprised her, considering she was among the Vampires, Werewolves and Witches. Saige was brought in first, her body hovering in the air, suspended inside what could only be described as a giant bubble. She watched in awe as the bubble drifted into the room, high above the heads of the crowd, and then descending to a platform in front of her. As soon as Saige landed, the bubble disappeared, a second one containing the still body of Brynn followed the same path. This continued until all six stood on the platform, their bodies held still by some invisible force.

"Meldron Merchant, you have been found guilty of conspiring to commit the murder of a protected creature. Theft and distribution of a forbidden substance. Aiding in the act of performing Black Magic. And aiding in the kidnapping of a Faction leader and Queen. Is there anyone among us who will speak on his behalf?"

Willow was impressed by the commanding way Thaddeus addressed the room. Dressed in a tailored suit and matching tie, he looked and acted like the lawyers she'd seen in movies.

"Do you have any evidence to dispute the findings of this Council or anything you wish to add to your defense?"

Mel cleared his throat, swallowing thickly before turning his eyes on Cerise. "Only to say how sorry I am for my actions. Looking back, even with the little I gained," his eyes shifting to Ophelia. "It wasn't worth it."

Silence covered the room as Meldron's confession hung in the air. Ophelia rolled her eyes in indifference, mumbling something under her breath loud enough only Mel could hear, who remained stoic despite the probable hurtful words.

"Saige, you have been found guilty in the murder of a guardian creature. Performing Black Magic after a previous conviction. The attempted murder of a Messenger by way of herbal toxicity. The kidnapping and attempted poisoning of a protected creature and heir to the reigning queen. Since this is your second offense, the Council has unanimously agreed you are a heightened risk to the community and your punishment shall reflect the severity of your crime."

Willow expected some clever comeback from the Witch who'd deceived her, however Thaddeus didn't allow her the opportunity to plead her case.

"Brynn, you stand accused of performing Black Magic after a prior conviction. Having a sexual relationship with a direct member of your bloodline. Attempted murder of a Messenger by way of herbal toxicity. The kidnapping and attempted poisoning of a protected creature and heir to the reigning queen. And murder of two Faction members, one by starvation and the second by beheading."

As Willow listened to Thaddeus list off Brynn's crimes, it hit her Viktor wasn't among the accused. She was certain she'd heard his name when the Council sat down to vote on the punishments.

"Ophelia Merchant, it is easier to list what you are not convicted of than those you are. However, none is greater than murder. The Council feels you are a danger, not only to the Faction community, but to human's as well after the blatant disregard you showed last evening."

Thaddeus turned his body toward Willow and the Council table, "Despite an extensive search of all the detainees, Ophelia was able to smuggle in a single vial of the elixir she used to create the original army for the King. The vial was discovered beside what remained of Viktor when the guards performed a routine check of the cells earlier this morning. A test of the concentration found it capable of turning more than one-hundred men. Two sets of fingerprints were found on the vial, that of Viktor and the second belonging to Ophelia."

Brynn dropped her head, her body quaking in what Willow assumed were sobs. Was it possible she was in love with Viktor? Or perhaps this was part of an act, another role she'd been playing for all of these years?

"Daragis, it was the Council's decision that with the original murder involving your father, you would have the authority to assign punishment."

Daragis rose from his seat, buttoned the top button on his suit jacket, and then turned to face Willow.

"Time and time again, these four have proven their disregard for not only Faction law, but for the precious life of its members. Ignoring the repeated warnings and tossing second chances out the window like yesterday's trash. My father was one of the most generous Dragons I knew, but even he had his limits. In my conversations with Garath, Black Magic was banished not only for its disastrous results, but for how it changed the owner of said magic. It created something so evil they wouldn't be welcomed even in the deepest pits of Hell. It is my wish they be destroyed by what they killed, their ashes placed in a vault protected by what was once known as the Messengers, now the Time Keepers."

With a simple nod of her head, Willow agreed with his request, hoping this would bring some peace to his troubled soul. Daragis bowed his head, then turned back toward the convicted, as members of the Council stood from their seats and joined him.

Willow expected a huge fireball to come shooting out of Daragis's mouth like a flame thrower, catching the four of them on fire, burning them alive as they screamed out in pain. But there was no fireball, not even a spark, only the skin at Daragis's neck shifting from the pink of his human form to the iridescent scales of what Willow assumed was his inner Dragon. The smell of a campfire came next, followed by four faces turning red as if they'd been out in the sun too long. Mel was first to slump over, the wisps of smoke rolling from his ears, followed by a bright glow seeping through his nose and mouth before his body crumbled into a pile of ash on the floor. Saige was next to fall, the small amount of hair left on her head sounding like a handful of firecrackers popping as her body fell to the floor. Brynn struggled against the invisible force holding her, smoke billowing from her mouth as she pleaded for mercy, her cries going unanswered. Ophelia kept her eyes on Larkin, repeating over and over how she'd done all of this for him. Her death took the longest, and Willow suspected the torture was intentional, but well deserved. As soon as Ophelia's ashes formed, Zarina was on her feet, her hands in the air, with Orifiel on her heels as four urn-like containers appeared on the ground beside each pile of ash. With a flick of her wrist, each pile of ash lifted in an arch from the ground, diving into the urns. Orifiel sealed each urn by waving his hand over the tops, a blue glow covering the urns before they disappeared, not a trace of them left behind.

"Larkin, you too stand convicted of more crimes than not. Have you anything to add to your defense?"

Larkin scoffed at Thaddeus's question, then tipped his head back before allowing a large ball of spit to fly from his mouth to the tip of Thaddeus's leather shoes. "Just kill me and get this shit over with."

Not missing a beat, Thaddeus pulled a handkerchief from his pocket, wiping the spit from his shoe, then crossing the room where he proceeded to shove the saliva-covered cloth into Larkin's mouth. "Would anyone speak in defense of the accused?" Thaddeus questioned the room, making his way back to the Council table. Adjusting his jacket as the murmur of laughter resonated from the spectating Factions.

"I would," Willow rose to her feet, a hush falling over the room. "Not in defense, but in request of a suitable punishment."

Willow stepped from the platform, walking with grace and determination to the table where the Council sat. "Despite the deception Larkin has demonstrated before this Council, his request for death is warranted, but not an equal measure for the crime. When he took the elixir, changing him into the creature he is now, it gave him not only the exterior of a warrior, but the heart and drive of one as well. In death, he will be free of the knowledge he is the son of a Troll, the Faction he despises so much it was his intention to destroy them. There will be nothing to remind him of his transgressions, or the lives he affected. Nothing to remind him of the pain and sorrow he left behind."

"And what do you suggest, Willow?" Daragis questioned, as Mathias reached out for her hand.

Turning to her left. "Arimas, you have a special ability, one I'm hoping you will feel comfortable sharing."

Arimas stood from his seat beside Kai, the beads in his dreadlocks clicking with his movements. "Larkin robbed me not only of my gifts, but he silenced my tongue for twenty years. There is nothing I wouldn't do to return the favor."

Willow lowered her head as Arimas returned to his seat. "It is my proposition to rebuild this city, cleaning up the streets and returning the lives of each Faction member to the harmony they enjoyed for so many years. It is my suggestion, however, to have a reminder of this day, of how a select few nearly destroyed the lot of us. If the Council agrees, I would ask Arimas to turn Larkin into a stone statue, one we would place in the heart of the city. Allowing us to remember, and Larkin to never forget. He will see each happy face, every celebratory event, the clean streets and the laughter, and the thriving businesses. But most of all, he will see the love he couldn't destroy." Willow squeezed Mathias's hand as she spoke the latter, her eyes boring into Larkin's to drive home her meaning. This idea had not been the result of a rash decision, but something she'd considered since learning the truth about Larkin.

Mathias raised his mate's hand to his lips, placing a kiss to her knuckles before letting it go and calling for a vote from the other leaders.

Willow returned to her seat, Orifiel sharing a proud smile, one she felt in the depths of her soul. Hushed conversations among the waiting Factions hummed in the room chasingaway any uncomfortable silence. While Willow and the rest of the room waited for the Council's decision, she analyzed the events of the meeting up to now. Leaning over toward her mother, gently whispering the question which had popped in her head. "Why did Dad have to seal the jars?"

Cerise kept her eyes on the serious faces of the Council, licking her lips, she tipped her head in Willow's direction. "Black Magic cannot be killed. If someone with enough magic and the know-how were to find the ashes, they could conceivably resurrect them and the magic they used."

A shiver ran down Willow's spine at the thought of Ophelia and her minions coming back to life, no doubt with a long list of retribution to pay.

"Don't worry, Willow. The Time Keepers would see if anyone was planning something and be there before anything could come of it."

"These Time Keepers, are they here, among the Factions?" Willow studied her mother's face, holding her breath as she watched a smile form across her lips.

"I'm looking at one now."

"I'm a Time Keeper?" Willow questioned albeit a little loud as several members of the Council glanced in her direction.

"You're an Angel, just like your father. The Gods gave this important task to their most trusted servants."

Willow allowed herself to lean back in her chair, the noise from the Council table barely registering as she considered what her mother said. She was one of the Time Keeper's, what that entailed, she didn't know. When Thaddeus rose from his seat and buttoned his jacket, she stowed away the worry, focusing instead on her plan to make the Factions strong enough to weather the storm if the unthinkable were to happen.

"The Council accepts your request," Thaddeus announced. "Larkin will spend eternity in the confines of a statue, but not made of stone, not with his Gargoyle ability to shift. We require he be encased in Barthenian steel."

Larkin roared his disagreement, as the Factions in the crowd jumped to their feet in cheers of victory. Arimas rose once again from his chair, his eyes glowing an odd green color, right arm extended with his fingers in the shape of a claw.

"Barthenian steel is an ancient metal no man or magic can penetrate." Cerise answered Willow's unspoken question, her eyes trained on Larkin as his body contorted, wings growing erect and his mouth gaping open. To any unknowing eye, Larkin appeared to be a simple statue found in any park in America.

"Lymrick, former Faction leader of the Fairies, your crime of treason holds a mandatory punishment of death, one served by any means the presiding Queen deems fit."

Willow could feel every eye on her, she hadn't considered a punishment for Lymrick. His betrayal in pretending to be someone else in order to get closer to her had affected her more than she cared to admit. With her mind completely blank, the panic began to rise in her chest.

"If I may say something." The tiny voice of Arcadia shattered through her indecision, like a lifeline to a drowning man. "I know the Fairy's have not earned our seat back, however we are still a Faction."

"Of course, Arcadia, you were asked to prove your worth to the Council. Go ahead. What do you have to say?"

Arcadia bowed her head to Willow, before cautiously approaching the Council table. "Some time ago, I was mated with a man my father arranged for me to meet. At first, I was against the possibility of mating with someone out of our settlement. However, the moment our eyes met, I knew it was real."

Coming to stand before Lymrick, Arcadia held her hands behind her back. "Two days before the mating was to take place, Lortis, the man I was to mate, and I took a walk so I could show him where we would be living. Everything was fine until Lymrick and his men passed us in their caravan."

Arcadia dropped her hands to her sides, stepping to less than a few inches from Lymrick's face. "You told your men to hold Lortis while you tried to rape me. When Lortis defeated those men, you sent the rest of them to hold him down while you severed his head from his shoulders. You laughed and turned those men on me, hitting and kicking me until I was unconscious. I woke up three days later with Lortis's lifeless eyes staring at me. I vowed then and there, someday I would avenge his death."

Without warning, Arcadia spun on her heels, crossing the room with determination until she stood before the Council table.

"I beg of you, please allow me the revenge I seek," her voice cracking as the first hint of a tear left her eye. "Allow me to take his life as he did my Lortis."

Willow moved her focus from the struggling face of Arcadia, to the shocked expressions of Rhea and two other women sitting beside her. How horrible it must be to have the love of your life taken from you, trapped in a world by a mad man. All the years Lincoln spent in his werewolf form, coming to visit her during the precious few minutes he could as a human. Arcadia would never have that, no Prince Charming at the end of her love story.

"No amount of magic can bring back your Lortis, but if revenge will help you sleep at night, then close your eyes and dream knowing you took Lymrick's last breath."

The sound of sniffling noses echoed around the room. Arcadia wiped the tears from her cheeks with the back of her hand, inhaling a deep breath before turning back in Lymrick's direction.

Pulling what looked like a bracelet from her wrist, she stood with determination, staring Lymrick in the face. "Can you release him, please. I have no intention of killing a man who is being restrained."

Orifiel looked to Willow, who nodded once but kept her focus on Arcadia. Raising his fingers casually in the air as if calling for a waiter in a restaurant, Lymrick stumbled several times before dropping to his knees before Arcadia.

"You time is over, Lymrick. May your soul never rest."

With a flick of her wrist, Arcadia tossed the bracelet at Lymrick, a flash of purple light lit up the room as Lymrick's vine covered body dropped like a stone to the floor. Thick, black branches covered his entire body, leaving his red face exposed, his eyes so wide Willow thought they might pop out of his head. White foam gathered in the corner of his mouth a second before his body went limp and his head rolled to rest at Arcadia's feet.

Several Trolls rushed in with a much larger urn, tucking the body of Lymrick inside, his head remaining under Arcadia's boot. Orifiel sealed the urn and handed Arcadia a silver bag, helping her place the severed head inside before setting it on fire. Every eye watched as the blue flames burned hot until there was nothing left. Arcadia returned to her seat as if nothing happened.

Thaddeus stood from his seat, making his way around the table and began addressing the Factions. Willow suspected this was the part where the closing statements would be made, and the Factions dismissed to return to their homes to rebuild. But she had a plan, one that started the moment she learned the truth.

"Faction leaders, if I could have your attention, please."

Willow stood from her chair as six sets of Council eyes stared back at her.

"I'm told New Orleans was once a great place for the Factions to live. With its history bathed in legends and mystery, it was the perfect place for the paranormal community to be themselves. Before I was born, this city was magical, filled with Factions who cared about each other and wanted more than anything to survive. One of our own tried to take that away and, had it not been for the careful planning of a bunch of people, they would have succeeded. Growing up, Evanora warned me to never venture far from home, and to especially stay away from New Orleans. She did this to protect me, knowing that today was coming. I may be able to see the past, but I'm powerless to change it. The future, however, is ours and it is my desire to give each of you the best fighting chance. It is with this hope; I give each of you a gift."

Willow separated the distance between herself and the shocked faces of the Faction leaders. Reaching into her pocket, she pulled out several crystal vials.

"Mathias, I have given you the gift, although inadvertently, of a heartbeat. You once told me how difficult it is for vampires to find their mates. My gift to the Vampire Coven is for the heart of every male to begin beating the moment they are near their mate." Willow leaned over, placing a kiss to Mathias's lips, the blue glow of her fingers tracing his heart.

"Daragis, your Faction is dying. With the inability to fly lifted, my gift to you is the power to mate with humans and giving them the strength to survive the birth of your children." Willow placed her fingers over his heart, the blue glow of her magic creating a warm sensation in his chest.

"Lincoln, you gave me a stone you said was a piece of the moon, a rock which has ruled your Faction since the moment you were created. It is my gift for the moon to rule you no more. Shifting is now your choice and not because of some rock." Willow placed her entire hand on Lincoln's chest, his spell needing a boost from her Angel magic.

"Azdren, your Pride has hidden in the shadows for far too long. Come, join up in the Quarter, and live without fear."

"Thaddeus, your Coven's power was stolen, businesses robbed from you and left many of you without a home to return to." Willow dragged her glowing fingers across his forehead. "I gift you prosperity, take back what is rightfully yours."

"Garath, the agreement between our families remains. I look forward to using my key to visit you in the Underworld, but I hope to see your handsome face around New Orleans every now and again. My gift to you is not only a safe return to your world, but for you to find the one who truly deserves you, who will wait for you until the end of time if she has to." Dragging her finger between his eyes, down his face and then circling his heart.

Willow knew the future was ever changing, evolving with each decision made. She could, however, do everything in her power to give them the tools to make the best possible outcome. Looking around the room, surveying each curious face, she knew this was where she was destined to be. Willow now understood, just when we think our story is over, we realize there is already a new chapter waiting to be written.

EPILOGUE

Five years later...

Willow tossed a handful of bird seed to the eager pigeons pecking the ground at her feet. Doing her part in filling the birds with enough sustenance they continue to decorate the statue behind her with their excrements. A smile teasing her face as she could practically hear Larkin's protest from deep within his metal prison.

With her bag of seed empty, Willow gazed at the businesses across the street, happy patrons leaving the stores with smiles on their faces and arms loaded with their purchases. It had taken the better part of a year to finish cleaning the streets of the Quarter. Despite a few squabbles over merchandising rights, the Witches were able to move back into their businesses, leaving the dark caverns they hid in behind.

Crossing the street, she shared her smile as she passed those patrons, relishing in the heat of the sun as it kissed her skin. Passing the antique shop, she glanced inside to see Tucker assisting a customer. Azdren took her gift to heart, allowing anyone in the Pride who was interested, to move to the Quarter. Tucker and Daragis discovered they shared a passion for rare antiques, entering into a partnership which has profited them both. Daragis left for Scotland recently, the call to find a mate too loud for him to ignore. He and his brothers will begin the process soon and Willow couldn't wait to meet the girl who won his heart.

Looking down the sidewalk, Willow's eyes land on Lincoln as he tossed his son high in the air, the child's laughter contagious and she couldn't help but join him. Rhea gave birth to their son nine months to the day of the curse breaking, but then held off for a couple of years before having anymore as she wanted to open a bakery, specializing in wedding cakes. Her confections are popular, however with the birth of their second child weeks away, Lincoln has stepped up to the plate, tying on an apron and creating some of the prettiest cakes she'd ever seen, next to Rhea, of course.

An advertisement painted on the back of a bench to her right brought her both sadness and joy. It's for a club at the end of the block, owned and operated by Garath. His return to the Underworld was short lived, his need to find a mate rivaling that of Daragis. Unlike his Dragon friend, Garath was fighting it, diving instead into making his club the most successful in the world. Willow knew it was only a matter of time before fate had enough and shoved his true love in his face. She only hoped the lucky girl had thick skin and heart big enough to love them both.

A honking horn pulled her attention from the misfortune of Garath to the taxicab driven by Arcadia. Willow waved at her friend as a new passenger climbed into the back of the car. The Fairy Faction had gone above and beyond in helping the Quarter come together, finding gaps in services which they found they enjoyed providing. Last year, a young Dwarf came to the city on holiday, his handsome face and pleasant demeanor attracting Arcadia's attention. While he lived in New York, the pair communicated every day. A more permanent relationship had been discussed, but with her role as a Faction leader, he understood her need to stay here. Still, Willow wouldn't be surprised if his long weekend trips turned into full time residency before long.

Turning the corner, Willow's eyes landed on Evanora's shiny red convertible and Zarina's new BMW-parked outside her mother's shop. The joy of seeing the trio of best friends reunited pushed away any ill feelings Willow may have had toward the secret they kept. After the sentencing, Evanora demanded Thaddeus go to Mel's garage and retrieve her beloved convertible, a wedding gift he'd given her new all those years ago. Willow learned how a spell was placed on the car, making her trip to New Orleans and the subsequent engine trouble a signal of her return.

Luprin and his people returned to the Quarter and played an active role in Council decisions. He and his brother took over Mel's abandoned garage, turning it from car repairs to custom bikes. People come from far and wide to purchase one of their unique creations.

Once the streets were clean, Willow began a project of her own, the restoration of the church Larkin trashed in his quest for dominance. It took the better part of two years, lots of compromises and a little help financially from Mathias before the doors were opened once more and a Priest was brought in. Willow took great pride in walking with Mathias every Saturday evening to the church, lighting a candle and kneeling beside him as he prayed.

On the rare occasion Kieran was in town, he too could be found at the altar, the rosary from his childhood clasped between his fingers as he asked forgiveness for all the sins he'd committed while on tour. Once Kieran learned of the gift she'd given every male vampire, he'd called her from the road, angry she couldn't have given him something useful like a better voice or a bigger dick. She'd laughed off his pseudo anger knowing her gift would come in handy very soon.

The bell over the door in her mother's shop chimed as she opened the door, the familiar scent of lavender greeting her, the sound of laughter filing her ears. Cerise and Zarina stood behind the counter, their faces red from jocularity. Evanora had her hand covering her mouth in an attempt to hide her laughter.

"Good morning, ladies." Willow called before closing the door behind her. The shop had changed completely since Ophelia first brought her to earn the money for car repairs. Her parents went immediately from the Council sentencing to the front door of this building, casting spell after spell to make it their home again. Her mother tossed out every bottle Saige had touched, spending weeks formulating new recipes. It was the right move as the shop was rarely empty. Luprin had come in and assisted with setting up an online store and they have a staff of six who fill those orders all day long.

"Good morning, sweetheart," her mother greeted through chuckles of remaining laughter. "Your father is waiting for you in the library."

Crossing the room, Willow placed a kiss to each lady's cheek, before venturing down the hall to the library. No matter the color of paint on the wall or thickness of the new carpet, Willow would always find peace in her parent's library.

Willow crossed the threshold to find Orifiel sitting at the end of the long table. Since returning, he'd taken over the library, having accepted the role as lead Time Keeper.

"Hey, Dad," placing a kiss to his cheek, Willow took the seat to the left of her father. As much as she enjoyed making love potions and elixirs with her mother, the responsibility of checking on the urns under the Time Keeper's watch had become her passion. The pair of them spent hours upon hours perusing ancient scrolls and slipping back in time to monitor the urns under their care. "Anything new? Larkin says hello."

Willow never imagined the kind of world which existed

behind the paranormal community. Factions upon Factions who desired the same form of harmony they created in the Quarter, were willing to pay great sums of money to come and learn how it was done. That's not to say everyone desired peace, some wanted closeness for their personal gain, giving Willow and her father more work than they could handle.

"Glad to hear prison hasn't dampened his spirits." Orifiel teased, leaning back in his chair, appreciating the beautiful woman his daughter had grown into. "Any news on the wind?"

In the days following the Council's sentencing, Arcadia asked for an audience with Willow. She'd felt horrid for showing up at her birthday party without a gift and wanted to right the wrong, so she taught Willow how to listen to the wind. Now, every morning as she fed the birds and checked on the seal placed on Larkin's statue, she listened as the wind brought her tales from around the world.

"Yes, actually, something about some missing Goblins in Ireland."

"I'm sure it's nothing. Goblins can be fickle creatures, and are known to overindulge, and then sleep for days."

"I don't know, Dad, it sounded serious."

"Well, we can always check it out after we have a look at the urns. However, I swore to that husband of yours I would have you back before lunch so he can sweep you away on a long overdue honeymoon."

Willow managed to keep Mathias and their wedding at bay until the church was complete. On opening day, the Quarter celebrated its rebirth by hosting the largest wedding since Orifiel married Cerise. The honeymoon had been rescheduled twice due to Faction business and Mathias refused to reschedule a third, threatening to kidnap his own wife.

"Listen, Willow, I know how much you love this community and would hate to see anything bad happen to it. Remember, we have measures in place to prevent anything like what happened to you."

Willow wanted to believe her father, but something told her there was more the wind was trying to tell her.

The End.

OTHER BOOKS IN THIS SERIES

TIME KEEPER TALES

Angel Kiss

Angel Awaken

Avenging Angel.

CODE OF SILENCE SERIES

THE BAD BOYS OF THE MAFIA.

Shamrocks & Secrets

Claddagh & Chaos

Stolen Secrets

Secret Sin

Secret Atonement

Buried Secrets Coming Fall 2019

Secrets & Lies Coming Winter 2019

SOUTHERN JUSTICE TRILOGY

WHEN THE GOOD GUYS FOLLOW THE BAD BOYS RULES. KU EXCLUSIVE.

Absolute Power

Absolute Corruption

Absolute Valor

STICKY-SWEET ROMANCE

Crain's Landing

JUSTICE

REVENGE REALLY IS BEST SERVED COLD.

Justice

HOSTILE TAKEOVER

A BILLIONAIRE ROMANCE

Hostile Takeover

ABOUT THE AUTHOR

Cayce Poponea is the bestselling author of Absolute Power.

A true romantic at heart, she writes the type of fiction she loves to read. With strong female characters who are not easily swayed by the devilishly good looks and charisma of the male leads. All served with a twist you may never see coming. While Cayce believes falling in love is a hearts desire, she also feels men should capture our souls as well as turn our heads.

From the Mafia men who take charge, to the military men who are there to save the damsel in distress, her characters capture your heart and imagination. She encourages you to place your real life on hold and escape to a world where the laundry is all done, the bills are all paid and the men are a perfect as you allow them to be.

Cayce lives her own love story in Georgia with her husband of eighteen years and her three dogs. Leave your cares behind and settle in with the stories she creates just for you.

Made in the USA
Columbia, SC
27 September 2021